A Wild Ride

Books by Jane Tesh

The Grace Street Mysteries
Stolen Hearts
Mixed Signals
Now you See It
Just You Wait
Baby, Take a Bow
Death by Dragonfly
Gone Daddy Blues

The Madeline Maclin Mysteries
A Case of Imagination
A Hard Bargain
A Little Learning
A Bad Reputation
Evil Turns

A Wild Ride

A Madeline Maclin Mystery

Jane Tesh

Savvy Press

First Edition 2020

Library of Congress Control Number: 2020935851

ISBN: 9781939113498   Trade Paperback
ISBN: 9781939113504   Kindle

Savvy Press
479 Beattie Hollow Rd
Salem NY 12865
www.savvypress.com
info@savvypress.com

Cover design: Fervor Creative

Printed in the United States of America

This book is dedicated to my good friends
Emily Cole and Linda Parks, who have been
through quite a few wild rides with me.

My thanks to Ellen Larson for editing
A Wild Ride and seeing it through all
its stages to Kindle and paperback.
My thanks, also, to Fervor Creative for
their excellent cover design.

Fly then swiftly and speed to the east,
Bravely determine all trials to bear.
Hunger and thirst, thorns and hard ways,
Smile through all pain while suffering pangs!

From *Die Walküre* (The Valkyrie) by Richard Wagner

CHAPTER ONE

I've always had a touchy relationship with my mother. She had one idea of how my life should be, and I had another. The fact that I'm a successful private investigator baffles her. But, as it turned out, this was one instance when she was glad I had some detecting skills.

***

Morning in the small North Carolina town of Celosia meant one thing: breakfast at Deely's Burger World, where Celosians went to hear the latest news, scandals, gossip, and rumors. According to the locals, Deely's Burger World had been a popular spot in town from its early days as an ice cream parlor. The counter tops were the original gray and white Formica. The silver stools had red plastic cushions, and the matching red plastic booths squished when you sat down and stuck to your legs in summer. The yellowed wallpaper had never been changed and displayed old ads for Coke and other colas long forgotten.

Things looked the same as always, but lately, at home and here at the diner, I'd noticed that Jerry had odd preoccupied moments that meant he was thinking of something I probably didn't want to know about. Oh, he was still cooking the best bacon biscuits and chatting with everyone, but there was a look in his warm gray eyes that usually meant trouble. There had also been a strange message on our answering machine the other day from a woman who called herself Sobbin' Susie:

"Just wanted to say hi, Jerry, from me and the gang. Things are rolling right along here. Thought you'd like to know."

Well, I wanted to know, that was for certain. Jerry had shrugged it off, saying he and Susie were friends but had never worked together. This didn't matter. Jerry's friends were a constant source of trouble.

I sat down at the counter. Jerry brought my breakfast and leaned over the counter to give me a kiss. "Expecting anything wild waiting for you at Madeline Maclin Investigations today?"

"As you know, business has been kind of slow, but it's only a matter of time before someone snaps."

"Let's hope it's more witches."

Former members of the Dark Rose Coven had figured in my last case. "I don't think Celosia has any more paranormal stuff going on."

"Oh, I'll bet something will turn up."

Behind us, the door to the diner swung open, and a voice called out in delight.

"Miss Parkland, as I live and breathe!"

Oh, no, I thought. *Another one of my rabid fans, the ones Jerry calls Pageantoids.* I turned to see a short skinny man with slicked back brown hair whose smile beamed as brightly as his loud Hawaiian shirt. It wasn't a Pageantoid. It was Jake Banner of the *Galaxy News Weekly.*

Jerry grinned at the man. "Jake, what are you doing here?"

Jake plopped himself onto the stool beside me, his blue eyes sparkling. "I've been meaning to look you up, but things have been unsettled in the Bermuda Triangle, and I just got back. How's it going, Madeline? I hear you and Jerry uncovered a coven round these parts. Sorry I didn't get the story on that."

For a brief time after I left the pageant circuit, I'd worked as a secretary at the *Galaxy*, Parkland's premiere tabloid, which is where I'd first encountered Jake and his boundless enthusiasm. "It was an unusual case," I said.

"No problem for you, I'll bet."

"What brings you to Celosia?" Jerry asked. "We're fresh out of weirdness at the moment."

"Something new and exciting, bud," Jake said. He turned his toothy smile to me. "Have I got a proposition for you!"

I couldn't imagine what he was talking about. "You want to interview me for the *Galaxy*?"

"Better than that. Your story would make a great YouTube show, and I am just the guy to produce it."

"A YouTube show?"

Jake spread his hands wide as if envisioning the opening credits. "*Madeline Maclin: Miss Detective.*" At Jerry's snort of derision, he laughed. "Okay, okay, we'll work on the title. But the potential for this is huge! You use your special set of skills to solve crimes, don't you? You've already solved, what, ten murders here?"

"Five, and I really don't think—"

"No, no, hear me out. We'll start with a social media campaign, get people interested. We can post all about your previous adventures. Then I'll follow you as you work on your next case, and we can show people how you do it. You'll get tons of subscribers. What do you say?"

I did not like this idea, at all. "Jake, I don't need anyone following me around with a camera."

"Oh, you won't even know I'm there." Again his hands danced in the air. "I am a shadow."

Jerry was enjoying this, but I had read Jake's "news" articles and was highly skeptical." Jake," I said. "I hate to tell you, but I haven't been riding in a UFO with Elvis lately."

He put a hand to his heart as if wounded. "This is totally on the up and up, Madeline. A completely true and unvarnished look at how a remarkable young woman such as yourself goes from beauty queen to successful detective. What's not to like about that? Basil's hoping to expand the YouTube channel for the *Galaxy*. Everybody's doing it."

"So your boss is all in on this idea?" Jerry asked.

"Yeah, he thinks it's great."

"Kind of a trial run, is it?"

"You could call it that. I prefer to say this show will be the flagship for an exciting new venture into the entertainment world." He snapped his fingers. "Wow! I got it!" His hands sketched a new title. "*Madeline Maclin: From Crown to Crime.* What do you say, Madeline?"

Looking into the man's beaming face with its eager expectant expression I realized how tough it was to turn Jake down.

"I'll think about it."

"Woo hoo, let me kiss the bride!"

I held up both hands to ward him off. "Settle down. I said I'd think about it."

"Is she always this cautious, Jerry?"

"We'll both think about it," he said.

"Can I start today, maybe get the backstory, see your office, that kind of thing? What kind of cases you got goin'?"

Unfortunately, I didn't have any cases at the moment, so I didn't have an excuse. Unlike Jerry, whose con man experiences taught him to always have a story ready, I wasn't good at spur of the moment fibs. Well, what harm could it do? Maybe a bit of You-Tube publicity would be good for my agency.

"Nothing very serious right now."

"Great! Let's go."

"My office is in the Arrow Insurance Building on Main Street," I said. "Let me finish my breakfast, and I'll meet you there." He agreed and dashed out.

"So what do you think about it?" Jerry asked. "Sounds like fun to me."

"I suppose it could be fun as long as he doesn't get in the way." I gave him a serious look. "Speaking of fun, is there something going on in Con World I should know about?"

He was instantly at his most innocent. "I no longer live in Con World. You know that."

"I have a feeling you visit from time to time."

He held up both hands. "If this is about Susie, I promise there is nothing new going on."

Hmm. What about something old? Before I had a chance to challenge him, my phone beeped and I glanced at the caller ID. It was my mother.

Her voice was, as usual, cool and direct. "Madeline, I wanted you to know that everything is all set for the gala."

My mother was on the board of the Parkland Museum of Art. A week ago, she'd called to let me know the museum was holding a gala as a fund-raiser. The gala committee had asked several prominent local artists to loan works for the event, and she'd told Letticia Booth, the museum director, that I wouldn't mind if *Blue Moon Garden* was included.

She loved including me in that "prominent local artists" category. *Blue Moon Garden* was my best work and currently on loan to the Parkland Museum of Art, located in my mother's town of Parkland, about thirty minutes from Celosia. I'd said that was fine with me.

It was more than fine. It was a complete turnaround from her usual behavior. She was a perfect example of How Not To Parent. Divorced, bitter, and self-involved, she tried to mold me into whatever ideal she thought pageants represented, and she ignored my wishes and refused to acknowledge any of my plans for my future.

Until now.

"I have tickets for you and Jerry," she said. "He does have a tuxedo and a black tie, doesn't he? This event is going to be very exclusive, you understand."

"I'll make sure he's dressed appropriately."

Her voice changed to the slightly accusatory tone I knew well. "Madeline, while I was at the club yesterday I ran into Billamena Tyson's mother. She said Billamena had been the victim of some sort of con job that you and Jerry sorted out."

"That's right."

"I didn't like the things she insinuated about Jerry. He wasn't involved, was he? And what about murders, Madeline? There haven't been any more murders in that little town, have there?"

"No, everyone's behaving themselves." I didn't dare mention Jake's new idea of *Madeline Maclin: From Crown to Crime*. She'd be overly excited and insist the YouTube show lean heavily toward my pageant career.

"All right, then." She ended the call.

"What's up with Cecille?" Jerry asked. "I noticed you didn't tell her about your new YouTube show."

"I'm sure Mom would prefer the crown part over the crime. She has gala tickets for us and hopes you have a plain black tie. Now, about what we were discussing earlier."

He gestured toward the kitchen. "I got orders piling up back there. Talk to you later, okay?"

"This isn't over," I warned.

CHAPTER TWO

Jerry's friends were a constant source of distraction. I'd taken care of Rick Rialto, clearing him of a murder charge during the making of the Mantis Man movie. He owed me. Honor Perkins, who wanted Jerry back as her partner in crime, had been a pest until I lied and told her I was pregnant. She agreed to leave Jerry alone so he could have the family he'd always wanted. Double-Dealing Derek, who forced Jerry to take part in a con, had been truly dangerous until Big Mike arrived on the scene.

Big Mike was the head of a shadowy crime organization, an organization Jerry had been recruited into after college. I didn't know much about him, but he'd taken care of Derek, leaving me in his debt. In debt to Jerry's sensei, the man who taught him all the tricks and cons. A favor, he called it.

Jerry had told me not to worry, that Big Mike was nothing if not fair. But I knew that when I least suspected it, a black Hummer would appear in the drive, and Big Mike would appear at my door. I'd have to take a mysterious package to China, or pretend to be a high class call girl to get the goods on some lowlife who'd dared cheat the big boss.

Jerry promised me he was getting out of the game, but this mysterious call from Sobbin' Susie made me wonder if another con was just around the corner.

***

Jake was waiting at my office door, taking pictures of the "Madeline Maclin Investigations" sign and the surrounding area. Despite his overly enthusiastic nature, Jake had helped me discover what had happened to Jerry's parents, and he'd also come snooping around when we were looking for Mantis Man, Celosia's Bigfoot. I unlocked the door and invited him in.

My office was small with a pleasant view of the neighboring yard. The walls had been paneled in light pine, but now gleamed with a mural I'd painted of yellow and green flowers. I'd brightened up the place by adding some personal items to the bookshelf, including a patchwork frog my grandmother had made, sea shells from the North Carolina coast and Bermuda, and small favorite paintings and drawings. My sketch of Jerry on the porch was one of my most successful. I'd managed to capture that impish grin and the light in his gray eyes.

Jake switched his phone to video mode and made a panoramic sweep of the room. Then he plopped down in the beige and green armchair I have for clients and aimed the phone toward me.

"Okay, now I want to hear how you decided to leave the pageant world and set up your own agency. You worked with Reid Kent in Parkland for a while, didn't you?"

"I worked next door to Kent and Ross. Not the best working environment." Not with Reid making snide sexist comments about my abilities. "When Jerry inherited the Eberlin House, we decided to move to Celosia. I solved a murder at the Miss Celosia Pageant, and things have improved ever since."

"Hard to get away from pageants, would you say?"

"Somehow there's always a connection."

"I like that. We could call your YouTube show *Pageant PI*, or *Runway to Murder*. Maybe even *Tiara of Terror*." He adjusted the volume on his phone. "You said you didn't have any cases right now?"

"Celosia's a small town. People are usually pretty calm."

My door banged open and a large woman charged in, sparks of anger flashing in her blue eyes.

"Madeline, I have to talk to you about Amanda!"

Jake stood and beamed at her. "Well, hello."

She stopped short and eyed him. "Hello. I'm sorry, I didn't

know you had a client, Madeline."

He offered his hand. "Jake Banner, *Galaxy News Weekly*. I'm not a client. I'm doing a story on Madeline."

"Joanie Raines," she said.

He gestured to the chair. "You don't mind if video this, Ms Raines? Unless it's a sensitive case."

"No, you're welcome to stay. I want everyone to know what sort of woman Amanda Price is."

In honor of Celosia's one hundredth birthday, the Women's Improvement Society decided to write an original outdoor drama, *Flower of the South*, the story of Emmaline Ross, a daring young pioneer woman and one of North Carolina's first vintners. The drama had been the brainchild of Amanda Price, my former client and a thoroughly unpleasant person, but when the other women in the group realized they had the money and therefore the power, they staged a coup and tossed Amanda out. To retaliate, Amanda wedged herself into the community theater in the neighboring town of Rossboro. Rossboro claimed Emmaline Ross and the entire Ross family, so they decided they should have a show about her and immediately started to create one. They called their show *Vines of History*. Now there were two outdoor dramas competing for bragging rights and valuable tourist dollars.

The light of battle gleamed in Joanie's blue eyes. She plopped herself into the armchair. "Make sure you get all this," she told Jake, who obligingly moved to keep her in the frame. Joanie flipped back her long brown ponytail, and let fly. "Madeline, you remember how scheming Amanda was and how she tried to take over *Flower of the South* and set herself up as the lead when everyone knows Emmaline was in her teens. Well, she's trying to do the same thing in Rossboro. The Rossboro Arts Council had everything worked out. *Vines of History* has a great script, much more historically accurate, and we have a great cast. There's even an amphitheater we can use. Then along comes Amanda. She sits in on all our meetings and has all these opinions and suggestions. She's trying to mount a hostile takeover, and the head of the Arts Council is too nice to tell her to shut up."

"Unless she's doing something illegal, I can't help you," I said.

"She's just so damn pushy. She seems to think she can buy her way in."

I sighed. Joanie had always seen Amanda as a threat to her own community theater career. "Remember Amanda only pretended to be wealthy. That's how the Women's Society got rid of her. They bought her out. Unless Amanda's suddenly come into a ton of money, you shouldn't worry."

"I'm afraid that's what's happened. The Rossboro Arts Council has a bigger theater budget than Celosia's, but Amanda could still take over. She's planning something, I know she is. She's been poking her nose into every inch of the Rossboro Little Theater from the costume shop to the box office. She's got no business doing that."

Jake caught my eye and grinned over his phone. He was finding this as ridiculous as I was.

"Well," I said, "if and when Amanda attacks, call me."

Joanie took my offer seriously. "Oh, I will."

"You know she likes to walk all over everyone to make herself feel important."

"That's true. At least she's not playing Emmaline."

"Are you?" This had been another sore point between Joanie and Amanda.

"The fellow who wrote our play came up with a brilliant idea," Joanie said. "We have this very talented young woman who plays Emmaline in the first scenes, and I play an older Emmaline looking back on my career. It's perfect. We even look alike. I know Amanda's seething that she didn't think of that. How's *Flower of the South* coming along? I hear they made some changes. Did they keep all of Jerry's songs?"

Jerry had written the musical score for *Flower of the South*. The new director had kept most of the music, but decided the script needed work. "From what Jerry tells me, they totally revamped the script."

"Do you think they'd mind if I came to a rehearsal?"

"I don't see why."

Joanie pushed herself out of the chair. "Thanks, Madeline. I'll keep you posted. Nice to meet you, Mr. Banner. You have my permission to post that video anywhere you like."

"Pleasure to meet you, Ms. Raines." He clicked off his phone, held the office door for her, and shut it behind her, his expression one of comical dismay. "*That's* the kind of thing that goes on around here?"

"Usually. I've found lots of overdue library books, too."

"Wow, *From Crown to Crime* is going to need some serious spice. Two women at odds over a play isn't really my line—unless she and Amanda get into a wrestling match." He glanced out the window at the distressingly ordinary sight of the neighbor children's swing set. "Is there anything, you know, supernatural going on? An outbreak of zombies, maybe, or some poltergeist activity? Jerry's not doing his séances anymore, is he?"

"He'd better not be."

Jake grinned. "Your house is haunted, though, right? The Eberlin House has quite a reputation."

"You can come see for yourself."

"Okay. I gotta check in with the boss first. I'll see you there."

Since my house wasn't haunted and packs of zombies weren't roaming the fields, Jake was certainly welcome to come to my house.

***

Since my house was about a mile from town, I didn't expect to see my friend and local poet Hayden Amry out that far, but to my surprise, there he was, ambling along the road. This was out of character for Hayden, who spent most of his time at his house writing, or working at Georgia's Books downtown. I slowed down and pulled up beside him. "Hi. Need a ride?"

He seemed disoriented. "Oh, hello, Madeline. No, I think I'll walk."

"Mind if I walk with you?"

"All right."

I parked off the road and joined him. Jerry and Hayden were almost the same height and size. Jerry's hair was a lighter brown than Hayden's, and both men had beautiful eyes. Jerry's were a warm gray. Hayden's were the color of the Caribbean Sea and at the moment, a bit glazed. He had on khaki pants and a white shirt with the sleeves rolled up. He looked tired and dusty.

"Sure you don't want a ride? I can take you home."

"I need to walk."

"Anywhere in particular?"

"No."

"Can I call Shana and tell her where you are?"

"Okay."

"He's where?" His wife Shana said in amazement when I called. "He walked all the way out that road? Is he all right?"

"He's fine." Hayden had stopped to lean over a rail fence and look at the fields full of wild flowers. The June weather was warmer and more humid than usual today. White clouds towering in the distance promised the chance of a thunderstorm later in the afternoon. "I'm going to try to convince him to come home with me."

"I'll be right there."

I put my phone in my pocket. "Hayden, I live just up the road. Would you like a glass of tea? We could sit on my porch for a while."

He turned his gaze back to me. I could tell he was having trouble processing what I'd said, so I repeated it. He blinked a few times as if clearing his vision.

"I'm not sure where I am," he said.

"We're almost to my house. It's pretty hot out here. Let's go find a cool place to sit."

He thought it over and then nodded. I guided him back to my car. He got in, and I drove the short distance to my driveway and up to the house.

When Jerry inherited the old rambling house, it looked exactly like a haunted house. But over the past months, with a lot of help from our local handywoman, and generous donations from Jerry's younger brother, Tucker, we'd transformed the shabby structure into a pleasant country home. The front porch no longer sagged, and the yard looked like a yard and not a weedfest. Jerry's Uncle Val, the former owner of the Eberlin House, had been an eccentric man who studied bats. I'd even gotten used to the fluttery little creatures that swooped and dived in the evening sky.

I parked under one of the large oak trees in the front yard. Hayden got out, moving as if sleepwalking. He took a seat in one of the rocking chairs on the porch. The squirrels put on a show chasing each other up and down the trees, but he paid no attention to their antics. I brought him a glass of tea and sat down in the chair beside him. After a drink and a few moments sitting in the shade, he seemed more coherent.

"You want to talk about what's bothering you?" I asked.

He rubbed his forehead. "I can't write anymore, Madeline. I can't think of a single thing."

"Maybe you're trying too hard."

"I was so certain my latest collection was perfect. I know it was perfect. I chose every word so carefully. But no one wants it. No one will ever see it."

"You can send it somewhere else, can't you?"

"It's pointless. No one wants it. I can't deal with any more rejection."

I knew something about rejection. My first art exhibit had been cruelly criticized by Parkland's leading art critic, and it had taken me a long time to get past the cutting remarks and paint again. So I didn't want to say things like, "Oh, you'll get over it," or "You have to ignore the negative reviews." I could still remember how that criticism stung, how I swore I would never put myself through such torture again. Hayden would have to find his own way through that kind of emotional minefield. I also knew he'd recently lost his mother and his pet ferret, Poltey. This had to be part of his problem.

Shana arrived within ten minutes, ran up the steps, and gave him a big hug. "Am I going to have to put a GPS on you?" Her tone was light, but her tawny eyes were worried. "What are you doing way out here?"

"I needed to walk," he said. "I didn't want to walk in our woods. It's better out here. There's more light."

"Well, that's fine, if you'll just let me know where you are."

"I'm sorry. I got a little turned around."

"You got a lot turned around." She propped on the porch rail, facing him, and pushed back her long red hair. "You know everything's going to be all right. You've been through this before. You can't let it overwhelm you."

"It's just so damn discouraging."

"Of course it is. And you know your anxiety level goes up if you don't take your medicine."

"*Twelve Leaves* is perfect. I know it is. You'd think with the success of *Glass Plums*, they'd want to publish more of my work."

"They will. You have lots more poems."

"I can't seem to finish them. They're like blocks of cement."

"I will buy you some dynamite."

Hayden looked at her and then began to smile. "I'm crazy, aren't I?"

"Pretty much."

"Madeline, what you must think of me."

"I've known you for a while," I said. "Remember all the ghosts Jerry and I have exorcized for you?" The Miss Celosia Pageant case had involved a young woman posing as a ghost to scare him.

"No ghosts this time. Just a bad case of writer's block. Cement block."

"You'll get through this," Shana said. "Then you can walk all over Celosia if you like, only please, please tell me where you're going. Our little town's not dangerous, but why take chances?"

Actually, I'd solved five murders in Celosia, so he needed to pay attention to Shana's warning.

"You're right," Hayden said. "I know I haven't been thinking clearly lately. I had a list of people to call to let them know about Mother, and I'm not sure who I called. I really didn't expect—I don't suppose anyone's really ready for that kind of thing."

Shana, who came from a loud, boisterous family that would probably tackle death to the ground and refuse to die, nodded in sympathy. I thought of my own mother and how I would miss her, despite our quarrels and differences.

"I'm so sorry about your mother, Hayden."

"Thank you," he said. "She enjoyed hearing about your adventures."

"What happened to Poltey?"

"The vet said he wasn't sure how old Poltey was. He stopped eating, and I found him dead in his cage one morning."

"That's too bad. I know he was your first pet." Mrs. Amry had been afraid of animals, so Hayden had grown up without even a goldfish.

"I told him we could get another ferret," Shana said. "Two, if he'd like."

"I'm not ready," Hayden said. "Maybe after everything settles down."

We heard the cheerful "Beep! Beep!" of a car horn, and a purple Gremlin with gold stripes came up the drive. Jake Banner parked the little car next to my light blue Mazda and hopped out, beaming, as usual. His phone was out and recording.

"This is a great location!"

He bounded up the porch steps and I introduced Shana and Hayden. "You're Shana Fairbourne, right? Author of *The Lustful Lady*? My wife reads your books. Hot stuff. Nice to meet you, and you, too, Hayden. What's your line?"

Not the most tactful of questions under the circumstances, but Hayden didn't flinch. "I write poetry."

"Yeah, so we're all writers here, that's cool. Do you two have a case for Madeline to solve?"

"She's helped us out in the past, but we don't have a mystery for her today," Shana said. "We ought to be going, Madeline. I'll call you later."

"How about a tour of the house?" Jake asked as she and Hayden waved good-bye.

I showed Jake the living room, which had been dismal and gray with plenty of cobwebs in the windows, but was now clean and light, the walls painted a peaceful sky blue, and the dark Victorian furniture replaced by a modern white sofa, glass coffee table, and crystal lamps on matching end tables.

Jake moved his phone to pan across the room. "Not what I expected. Nice, really nice."

Then we went to the kitchen, the one room that hadn't needed a lot of remodeling. Uncle Val's appliances were in good shape, and we'd kept the sturdy white wooden table and chairs, dressing them up with a blue and white tablecloth and skipper-blue cushions. The white floor had matching patterns of blue leaves, and lacy white curtains billowed in the breeze from the open windows that lined the back of the kitchen.

"Great view," Jake said, holding his phone up to the windows.

It was a great view, green and gold fields and the woods that bordered our land. Birds chirped at the feeder I'd hung in one of the trees. Several volunteer sunflowers and zinnias poked up from the untidy flowerbed I kept meaning to weed.

The only other room I agreed to show was upstairs. Jerry's Uncle Val might have used the second floor parlor for his study, but now it was my studio. Once I cleared out the heavy old-fashioned furniture and removed the thick gray draperies, the room filled with plenty of natural light. I kept my easel set up near the widest window, and finished work was propped up around the room like a private gallery. I had commissioned landscapes and portraits ready to go, and my current projects hanging on the far wall.

Jake walked around, videoing the pictures. "Hey, these are pretty good. Maybe *From Crown to Crime* will bring in more customers." He clicked off the video. "Too bad you don't have a little mystery going. Maybe the artist angle would be better."

"That would be fine with me."

He snapped his fingers. "I forgot! My niece Valerie did a story on you for the *Herald* several months ago. Not a bad article, if I recall correctly. Yeah, so that's been covered. We'd better stick with *From Crown to Crime* and hope something happens." He put his phone in his pocket. "Okay, I'm going to get started on your channel. Call me the minute somebody kills somebody."

I promised I would, and he hurried away.

***

For dinner, Jerry made baked spaghetti and we ate on the porch. For a large part of the summer, he'd been writing, playing, and conducting the music for *Flower of the South*, but to his relief, his presence was no longer required at rehearsals. As I'd mentioned to Joanie, the new director kept the songs Jerry had written and enlisted more local musicians to play in the orchestra. Jerry had taught a promising high school pianist named Sandy how to conduct. He'd jumped at the chance to pass that responsibility on to someone else. As I'd figured, writing silly songs for community theater productions was wearing thin, but at least it had kept him occupied for a while.

Tonight, his gaze strayed to the window. I knew he wasn't looking at the peaceful fields, or the dark woods beyond, or the antics of the little bats that fluttered above the trees. Now was the time for some answers.

He caught me looking at him. "What?"

"Were you back in Con World?"

"No."

I raised an eyebrow, and he grinned.

"Yes. Sort of."

"Are you sure you've told me everything about Sobbin' Susie? What did she mean by 'Things are rolling right along here'?"

"Something she's got going with Speedy Sam."

"Jerry."

He laughed. "Just kidding."

I really wanted to believe him. "So Susie doesn't need your help to roll right along."

"Nope. Actually, I was thinking how Jake will manage to inject the paranormal into *From Crown to Crime*. He's really good at that kind of thing. Don't be surprised if he discovers you're in tune with the spirit of Agatha Christie."

"I think this YouTube idea has its advantages," I said. "Jake is quite a character, and *From Crown to Crime* could be fun. I can't really turn down extra publicity for my agency."

I started to tell him about Jake's reaction to Joanie Raines and her continuing feud with Amanda Price when my phone rang. It was Shana calling to thank me again for my help and to ask if Hayden could stay with us while she was on a book tour.

"This should be my last trip for the month," she said. "I was considering cancelling because Hayden's anxiety has gotten worse, but if you two can keep an eye on him and make sure he takes his pills, I might go, but I don't want to inconvenience you in any way."

"No problem," I said. "I don't have any cases right now. He can move in with us while you're gone."

Her voice sounded relieved. "Thank you so much. Even though you caught all the ghosts, he still worries about our house being haunted, and with everything else that's going on in his life right now, I'd feel better knowing he was with people."

"Hayden's going to stay here while Shana's on tour," I told Jerry after I ended the call. "Has he said anything to you about ghosts?"

"No ghosts, no monsters."

I finished the last bite of spaghetti and gave the chef my compliments. "Now, back to what we were talking about."

"Ghosts and monsters?" he said hopefully.

"No, your friends."

"Mac," he said, "I promise you nothing is going on right now."

"Right now, you say."

He grinned. "When did you become so suspicious?"

"You forget I am Madeline Maclin, Private Investigator. Nothing escapes me."

"I'll remember that," he said.

I had to be satisfied with his answer, but he and I both knew I was not going to let this go.

CHAPTER THREE

Jerry and I did a little investigating of our own that night, and I was sound asleep when my phone rang Wednesday morning, jarring me awake. My bedside clock said eight forty-five AM.

I checked the caller ID. It was my mother again. What on earth? "Hi, Mom, what's—"

She interrupted me, her voice on the rise. "Madeline, there was a break-in at the museum. All the paintings for the gala are gone! I was in charge, so I'm responsible. What am I going to do?"

Oh, my God. "Okay, calm down," I said. "Tell me exactly what happened."

"I came in this morning and the art work was gone! I immediately called the police. Someone stole the paintings, including yours! I'm so upset I can hardly breathe!"

I took a quick gulp. "Where are you, Mom? Is anyone with you?"

"I'm at home. After the police questioned me, they said I could go. I don't know what I'm going to do!"

"I'll be right there. We'll settle this, don't worry." I ended the call and elbowed Jerry awake. "Someone broke in and stole the paintings for Mom's gala, including *Blue Moon Garden*. We need to get to Parkland right away."

***

Parkland was only a thirty minute drive from Celosia, but it seemed much longer. The thought of *Blue Moon Garden* hanging in some crime lord's den, or worse, torn up for the canvas and frame, made me sick. On the way, Jerry called Celosia's chief of police, Gus Brenner, to ask if he'd heard anything about the crime and who we might contact at the Parkland Police Department. The chief said he'd get whatever details he could for us and to talk to his friend Jordan Finley in Parkland. I hoped Finley would let me in on the case, but I had my doubts. Chief Brenner and I had a good cooperative relationship, but then, I'd proven myself useful. Even though I'd once worked as an investigator in Parkland, Finley didn't know me or what I could do. This was going to be a hard sell. But my main concern was my mother.

Mom met us at the door of her large French cathedral-style home. My mother was a slim fashionable woman who favored black and white, but for the first time in years, she looked old and worn. She didn't hug me, but gripped my arm as she led me and Jerry into the living room.

"This is a nightmare. You wouldn't believe the phone calls I've been getting! This gala is a huge event. My reputation is on the line."

I sat her down in one of the plush white chairs. "Let me get you something to drink, and we'll figure out what to do."

Once she'd calmed a little, she was able to tell us more. "All ten paintings were taken, and someone left an awful little note!"

"You found a note?"

"No, but when I went to tell Letticia about the paintings she was sitting at her desk, and I'd never seen her so pale. She had a little piece of paper in her hand, and her hand was shaking. I told her what had happened, and she said, 'Then that explains this.'"

"What did the note say?"

"Oh, I can't remember exactly what it said. Something about real artists being ignored and the museum would get what it deserved. Then the police came, and Letticia gave them the note. The police said no windows were broken, no doors forced open. They said it looked like an inside job, and then they looked at *me*! Can you imagine me writing a threatening note? And why would I steal paintings I can easily afford? What would I do with them, display them here in my house? That's madness. Besides, none of them would go with my décor."

"Jerry and I are going to talk to the police and we'll come right back," I said. "Are you going to be okay by yourself?"

"Of course I am. I've been by myself for twenty-five years."

That sounded more like the mother I knew.

Jerry and I drove to the police station. I explained that I was Cecille Maclin's daughter and that Gus Brenner of the Celosia police department had suggested I talk with Jordan Finley. We were escorted to Finley's office.

Officer Finley was a large square-shaped man with a stiff brush of black hair and the same shrewd blue eyes Chief Brenner had. Shrewd blue eyes must be standard police issue. He shook hands with me and with Jerry and we all sat down. "Gus tells me you're a private investigator, Ms. Maclin. How are things in Celosia?"

"Busier than you'd expect. What can you tell me about the break-in at the Parkland Museum of Art?"

He consulted his computer screen. "We received a call from Cecille Maclin at eight thirty this morning that ten paintings were missing. My officers and I spoke with Mrs. Maclin, as well as the docents who were there, and Letticia Booth, the museum director. I understand one of the paintings was yours."

I was surprised my voice was steady. "Yes, my best one."

"We're doing everything we can." He slid some pictures across his desk. "Fortunately, we have some photos taken from last week when the *Herald* did a story on the gala. Which one is yours?"

I pointed to the familiar swirls of blue and silver. "This one."

"Do you recognize any of the others?"

Besides *Blue Moon Garden*, the stolen paintings included a modern piece in bright red and yellow, another modern piece done in pastels, a fine seascape, two beautiful mountain paintings, a graceful study of willow trees, a dramatic rendering of a forest fire, and two rough yet powerful portraits, one of an old man and one of an old woman. "Yes, I've seen all of these."

"Do you have any idea who might have done this?"

"No," I said. "My mother seems to think she's a suspect. Is she?"

"We're questioning everyone who had anything to do with the gala, but at the moment, she doesn't fit the profile. Right now, we're planning to interview anyone connected with the museum."

"What about surveillance footage?" I asked.

"Unfortunately the thief or thieves knew how to disarm the security system, including surveillance cameras." He gave me a measuring glance. "Ms. Maclin, I know you want to be involved, but it would be best if you let us handle this investigation."

"Yes, but I could be useful."

"I understand you've had some success in Celosia, but this is Parkland. We have our own resources and plenty of people to work this case."

I gave it another try. "Officer Finley, it's my mother and my painting we're talking about."

That did not change his mind. "Being too close and too emotionally involved can be a distraction. Leave this to us. If you discover anything or have any other insights into this case, you should let us know immediately, but please don't go charging around town getting in the way."

Well, I know about the note you haven't mentioned, I thought. But there was nothing else to say but "Thank you." Jerry and I left.

On the way back to my mother's house, we discussed what we could do. Although I'd grown up in Parkland, it wasn't my territory, and I didn't know where to go to get the instant information I usually picked up at Deely's. But I wasn't going to let this stop me from finding my painting.

"That note sounds like somebody's not happy," Jerry said.

"Yes. I need to talk to Letticia and find out exactly what it said. But let's get back to Mom first."

Once more, Mom met us at the door. "What did the police say? Are they going to let you work with them? Are you on the case?"

Are you on the case? Words I never thought I'd hear her say. Ever since I'd given up pageants my mother had derided and ignored my chosen profession. Now that she needed my help she was all about it. So I decided to take advantage of this opportunity.

"I'm on the case, Mom."

***

Mom insisted we didn't need to stay. Before we left, I looked up the information about the gala on the Parkland Museum of Art's website and the *Parkland Herald* to get a list of the artists and a list of patrons of the arts who had been invited.

"I don't see why you would think any of them know anything about the theft," she said. "This gala was to showcase local artists, like you, and although it was open to the public, all our special guests are people who have an interest in supporting local talent." She rubbed her forehead as if her head hurt. "I can't answer any more questions today, Madeline. I'm too upset. I'm going to call my doctor and get something for my nerves. This is simply awful. You have no idea."

"All right. Take it easy today. I'll call you as soon as I know something."

I wanted to say of course I had an idea. I had many ideas, none of them happy. Thinking of my missing painting made me so angry and frustrated. My mother wasn't an artist. She was the one who had no idea. Then I gave myself a mental shake. I could paint another *Blue Moon Garden*, couldn't I? It might not be as spectacular as the first, but it wasn't impossible to recreate. I had photos to work from. Still, I wasn't going to let someone get away with this.

Mom let me give her a good-by hug and then hurried us out and locked the door behind us.

"We'll find your painting, Mac," Jerry said as we got into my car. "We'll find all of them, and if necessary, we'll steal them back."

I hadn't thought of the con artist angle. "Does this seem like something your people would do?"

"I've heard of cons where valuable paintings were replaced with forgeries, or there was something even more valuable taken, and the theft of the paintings was a diversionary tactic. Has your mother riled anyone lately?"

"She riles people all the time."

"This might be someone's way of getting back at her."

I took out my list of artists. Besides me, there were six names. The only one I recognized was Tully Springfield, whom Jerry and

I had met before. I had a lot to think about, and it didn't help that Jake had heard the news and called, his voice brimming with excitement.

"Talk about timing! One of those stolen paintings is yours, isn't it? 'Tonight, on a special episode of *From Crown to Crime*, ace investigator Madeline Maclin searches for her own artwork tragically ripped from the Parkland Museum of Art. This time, it's personal.' When do we start?"

I took a deep steadying breath. "The Parkland Police are in charge of this investigation, Jake."

"Yeah, but you never let the police stand in your way. You've got a plan, right?"

"I don't exactly have a plan." I looked to Jerry for help.

Jerry was enjoying this. "Tell him we suspect it was the Phantom of the Museum."

I rolled my eyes in exasperation and spoke to Jake. "My first stop is going to be the museum. You can meet me there."

"Okay, Basil wants me to check out a possible werewolf sighting on Parks Street, so let me take care of that first."

"Sounds good." I ended the call. "The Phantom of the Museum? Seriously?"

"He would love it. So would I, actually."

"I don't think we're going to encounter anything supernatural on this case," I said.

"Don't be surprised. Jake thinks all the Fairweather brothers have an affinity with the supernatural."

One of Jake's crazier theories about the fire that killed Jerry's parents was that Mr. Fairweather had been trying out a spell that sent blue flames everywhere. Apparently, Jerry, his older brother Des, and his younger brother Tucker had all been hit by these magical flames which made them receptive to spirits. Des was furiously opposed to this theory, Jerry laughed it off, and Tucker had been too little to remember any of the incident.

"Well, if Jake comes up with a motive for this theft, supernatural or not, I'll believe it," I said.

***

Jerry said if I'd take him by his friend Del's pawn shop in Pot Luck Alley, he'd ask Del if he'd heard anything about the paintings, so after dropping him off, I called Letticia. She said I could stop by any time. I was fired up and ready to go when my phone rang. It was Jake.

"Okay, werewolf turned out to be somebody's exceptionally shaggy Saint Bernard. I am ready to go sleuthing with you today. Parkland is my beat, and all doors are open to me—even the ones that need a little extra push. If you're worried about me scaring off witnesses, I'll stay in the car with my zoom lens and trusty listening device. I've got all the latest gadgets, even a wristband audio recorder that looks like a smart watch. Really cool. Where do we start?"

"I'm going to start with the museum director," I said. "Could you scope out the museum and talk to the employees? Find out if anyone saw or heard anything that might help the case."

I was glad to hear this idea appealed to him. "Yeah, and I could look around the place for clues. Are you heading over there now?"

"Yes. I'll see you there."

"Woo hoo!" he said. *"From Crown to Crime* is on the move!"

CHAPTER FOUR

Letticia Booth met me at the door to her office in the Parkland Museum of Art. Letticia was a severe-looking woman dressed in black, her silver hair in a tight bun. Today, a few strands had escaped that perfect bun, which told me Letticia was extremely upset.

"Dear me, Madeline, I cannot tell you how sorry I am about *Blue Moon Garden*. We will do everything we can to recover it. Please have a seat."

I sat down in one of the plum-colored chairs in front of her desk. Letticia's office was a large airy room that could easily have been a little gallery in itself. The dominant colors were plum and gray. Black and white photographs of flowers decorated the walls. Three short Greek columns sat in front of the window, each one displaying an unusual piece of sculpture, a graceful nautilus shell, a frozen flame, a flower changing into a child.

"It wasn't your fault, Letticia."

She sat down behind her desk. "Oh, but I feel as if it is."

"My mother said you found a note."

"On my desk this morning." She took a piece of paper from the top drawer and slid it across the desk to me. "It's a copy. The police have the original. They hope they can get fingerprints."

The note said, "Ignore the real artist and this museum gets what it deserves."

"The real artist. That could mean several things. Maybe a forgery? Maybe someone who felt underappreciated? Or someone whose work wasn't accepted for the gala?"

"I can't really imagine who would do such a thing."

I took out my list of gala artists and my list of patrons of the arts. I placed both on the desk facing her. "Have you had any problems with any of these people?"

Letticia stared at the lists and then at me for a long moment. I thought she was going to refuse, and then she said, "Of course! I'd forgotten you're a private investigator. We had the *Herald* do a story about your duel careers. Why didn't I think of it? I'll hire you to solve this."

I was going to solve this anyway and find my painting, but being officially hired would be a plus. "I'd be happy to take this case."

She took another long moment and then leaned forward and clasped her hands together on her desk as she looked at the list of the gala artists. "It can't be any of these artists."

"But one of them might know something," I said.

She set that list aside and looked at the second list, the one of invited guests. "As for our patrons, everyone I spoke with was excited about the gala and had pledged to support the museum, so you can probably eliminate them."

It was clear that Letticia did not want to suspect her wealthy patrons. "I'd like to talk to your employees, as well, especially the ones on duty last night," I said. "The police told me the security system had been disarmed. Who would have access to it, or know how it works?"

"I know how it works, of course, and the employees who close the museum every night have the responsibility of making sure the system is on." She looked at the list. "Daniel Kimbro is in charge of the schedule."

"Thanks," I said. "I'd like to have a look at the room where the gala was going to be held."

"Yes, of course."

She led me down the hall to a large gallery. A "Closed" sign was propped on an easel outside the door.

Letticia motioned me in. "The police have finished examining the room, but we didn't want any of our museum visitors wandering in here until we'd had a chance to put things back in order."

The walls of the event room were—sadly—empty. I was certain the police had gone over the room thoroughly, but I appreciated the chance to look around.

Letticia stood by the door and watched as I inspected the room. There wasn't much to inspect. No bloodstains, no pieces of torn clothing, no buttons or fibers.

"Letticia, is there anything else you can tell me? Anything at all out of the ordinary recently?"

She took a deep breath, as if making a decision. "Madeline, several odd things have happened lately. Since this is your area of expertise, you might see some connection to the break-in."

"What kind of things and how odd?" I asked.

"About a month ago, the museum missed the deadline for a very important grant. This has never happened before. I am always extremely careful about getting all the correct paperwork in long before the deadline, but in this case, our proposal was never received."

"Did you do all the work yourself, or did someone help you?"

"Two of our board members, Doug and Dawn Elmore, were on the grant committee. They helped write the grant."

I made a mental note to add board members to my list. "What else?"

She pushed back a wayward strand of her silvery hair. "This is quite embarrassing, but last fall, the museum paid a lot of money for a painting that turned out to be a fake. Again, something that had never happened before and again, something that was my responsibility. We were very lucky that Tully Springfield, one of the local artists, discovered the forgery when he brought in his paintings for the gala."

"I know Tully. I'll check with him."

"And the other thing is not as important, but it's still seems odd to me. Every little thing that goes wrong now makes me think twice. A shipment of interactive playground equipment for our new children's exhibit failed to arrive. When I called to inquire about the order, the company said the order had been canceled. I didn't cancel the order. No one in my office cancelled the order. I reordered, of course, but the equipment will arrive too late for our exhibit. We had to reschedule everything." She gave me a worried glance. "This break-in and disruption of our major fundraiser could be the last straw, Madeline. My job and my reputation are on the line. If things continue to go downhill, the board will have every right to replace me."

"Is there anyone who would be happy to see that happen?" I asked.

She looked startled. "Are you asking if I have any enemies?"

"There could be someone who wants your job."

"I can't imagine who that might be—if that's what this is all about."

"Let me look into these incidents," I said. "I may be able to find an answer."

***

I left Letticia's office with my retainer and my lists. Jake met me in the foyer.

"I talked to lots of people, but nobody saw anything," he said. "What did Letticia Booth say?"

"Nothing helpful about the theft. But plenty about other odd happenings at the museum. She seems to be at the center of a lot of problems. And a note was found on her desk."

"A note! Even better. What's it say?"

"'Ignore the real artist and this museum gets what it deserves.'"

"A full-on mysterious threat. Fantastic!"

I didn't mind that Jake tagged along while I spoke with the museum volunteers. Three were on duty, all earnest women in their late sixties who were concerned about the break-in. Two of them knew my mother and expressed their dismay that my painting had been stolen. They'd all gone home at eight that night when the museum closed. "Who has a key to the museum?" I asked.

"Letticia, of course," one woman said. "She's usually here first thing every morning to open the museum. I think one or two of the board members has one."

"She leaves at five," another woman said. "Daniel is in charge of locking up at night. He assigns one of us to help him check the security system so we can make sure it's on."

"Who was with him last night?"

"You'll have to ask him," she said. "That's his desk over there."

No one was at the desk.

Jake spoke in an undertone. "Reckon he took the paintings and is half way to Vegas?"

"He might be in the men's room," one of the docents said.

Mr. Kimbro had indeed been in the bathroom, and returned, smiling. He was a bright-eyed young man rocking both a soul patch and a man bun.

"Daniel," the docent said, "these folks are here about the break-in."

His smile faded. "I can't believe something like this happened to our museum. What can I do for you?"

"Mr. Kimbro," I said. "I believe you were responsible for locking up the museum last night and making certain the security system was on."

"Yes, ma'am," he said, "and I can assure you, it was on when I left. One of the other docents was with me. Let me check and see who that was." He sat down at his desk and consulted his computer. "Ronelle Abbott. She's working the front desk this morning if you want to talk to her."

"So you have a key and Letticia has one. Who else has a key?"

Again, he looked up the information on his computer. "Besides Letticia and myself, board members Roxanna Deluca, Doug Elmore, and Cecille Maclin."

"And you have yours?"

He showed me the ring of keys on his belt and indicated a silver key. "Yes, ma'am, I keep it right here."

I thanked Daniel, and on our way out, Jake and I stopped by the front desk. Ronelle Abbott, a tiny elderly woman nodded vigorously when we asked if she'd helped Daniel lock the museum last night. "Oh, yes, we always double check. The museum was locked up tight and the little light was blinking to show the system was working." She frowned at Jake, who had his phone out. "Are you recording me, young man? I'll thank you to turn that off."

"Yes, ma'am," he said with a grin. He put the phone in his

pocket. "My apologies."

She turned to me. "Was there anything else you needed to know?"

"No, thank you," I said.

"We've got some excellent video," Jake said as we left the museum. "Except for Ms Ronelle. Some people are touchy. Just so you know, if we run into a reluctant witness or suspect, I can keep recording."

"You can record through your pants?"

He held up his wrist. "I told you about this gadget, right? This ain't no ordinary watch. I got audio, at least. And look. This handy little button calls the police. Lets them know your location and everything. You never know when you might need backup. The tabloid business is pretty risky."

"That's good to know."

"Too bad there's not a pageant connection to all this. Works better with the theme." He checked his watch. "I gotta get back and show Basil what I've got so far, plus he wants me to check out some Elvis sighting. I'll call you."

***

While Jake was fun to be around, I didn't need him to accompany me to Doug and Dawn Elmore's neighborhood. I got in my car and drove to Parson's Creek.

The Elmores lived in a brand new golden brown log cabin, so new the logs looked like plastic. There were shiny light brown rocking chairs on the porch, a wreath of daisies on the door, and a little wooden sign decorated with a rainbow that said, "There's No Place Like Home." Both Elmores came to the door and introduced themselves. They were short and stout with beaming faces. Their little black terrier ran around me in frantic circles, yapping excitedly.

"Dixie, calm down," Dawn said. "You'll have to excuse her. She does this to everybody."

"That's okay," I said, as Dixie banked off the side of the house and whirled around me again. "I won't take much of your time. It's about the break-in at the museum last night."

"Are you with the police?" Doug asked.

"No, my name is Madeline Maclin, and I am a private investigator based in Celosia. But I'm also an artist, and my painting was stolen, too."

"Horrible news," Dawn said. "The whole thing is horrible. Oh, Dixie, for heaven's sake, settle down."

Doug reached for the dog. "Here, let me take her out back." He managed to wrangle Dixie and carried the squirming dog into the house.

Dawn watched him go and then turned back to me. "You said you were a private investigator. Are you trying to find the paintings?"

"Yes," I said. "But I also wanted to talk to you and your husband about the grant proposal that missed its deadline."

Her cheerful face fell. "Oh, that was such a mess. We were absolutely sure we got that in on time."

"Did you email it? Fax it?"

"We mailed it the old-fashioned way. The Hester Fulton Memorial Museum Grants and Bequests is known for its generosity and also known for being a stickler for the way things always used to be, if you know what I mean. The remaining member of the Fulton family must be a hundred years old."

"So you took it to the post office?"

"We left the envelope on Letticia's desk with the few other pieces of mail that were supposed to be picked up that day. That's the last anyone saw it. Doug and I felt awful about missing the deadline. You can probably guess the Fulton Grants and Bequests doesn't let you reapply."

Which meant anyone with access to Letticia's office could have taken the grant envelope off of her desk. "Let me ask you something else," I said. "To your knowledge, did any of the artists represented at the gala have any competitors? Was there anyone who was left out, who maybe felt they were a better artist?"

She thought a moment and called over her shoulder to her husband. "Letticia's son made a fuss, didn't he, Doug?"

Doug came back out, shutting the door on Dixie's protests.

"What did you say?"

"Letticia's son, Zeke. No, it's Zack. Zack Turner. Wasn't he upset because he couldn't be in the show?"

"He doesn't paint," Doug said. "Does some kind of odd modern art sculptures in glass and rocks. The gala was featuring local painters."

"I suppose Letticia thought she'd be accused of favoritism if she made an exception," Dawn said.

"Does he live around here?" I asked.

"Got a place down near Applestone."

I'd heard of Applestone, a small artists' community not far from Parson's Creek.

"Letticia's got more things to worry about than her son and his rocks," Doug said. "Not only this business with the gala, but earlier this month, we found out we had a forged painting in the museum. The budget really took a hit on that mistake."

"Are these things likely to impact her position as director?" I asked.

"I don't think so," Dawn said.

Doug wasn't as sympathetic. "The board is going to have to take a good long look at her record."

There was a crash from somewhere in the house. "Oh, that dog," Dawn said. "Let me go see what she's into now."

I thanked the Elmores and went to my car. According to my GPS, Applestone was about three miles away. That would be my next stop.

***

Zack Turner reminded me of a scarecrow, tall and lanky, with straw-like hair. His barn studio in Applestone down at the end of a dirt road was surrounded by piles of stone and glass and strange blank-faced statues like a little garden of Easter Island heads. Zack Turner was hammering on another piece of stone. He stopped and pushed his safety glasses up onto his haystack of hair. At my question, he admitted he'd been annoyed when he couldn't take part in the gala.

"I guess I understand where my mother was coming from. The committee wanted only paintings for this gala of theirs. But don't they realize some collectors prefer sculpture? My work would've elevated the entire event to another level."

It sounded to me as if Zack Turner considered himself a "real artist." "You heard that the museum was robbed."

He pulled off his work gloves. "Yeah, too bad for them."

"One of the paintings was mine."

He grimaced. "Oh. Sorry about that."

"That's why I'm especially determined to find out who did this. Any information you could give me would be helpful. Besides yourself, were there any other artists who wanted to show at the gala and were turned down?"

"Phoebe Deluca."

"Deluca? Is her mother Roxanna Deluca? Isn't she on the museum board?"

"Ironic, isn't it?"

"What sort of art does Phoebe do?"

"The most amazing wire creations incorporating found objects. Her studio's just down the road. We can walk from here."

Phoebe's studio was an old barn attached to a small cottage. A battered white Camry filled with trash and boxes of odd items was parked in the side yard, the trunk open to reveal either yard sale bounty or curb side treasures. Zack led me around to the back door past a small fish pond filled with brackish water. A young woman looked up from a wad of old coat hangers and twine. Part of a baby stroller and two large deer antlers hung in the twine. She was blond and sweet-faced and wore a sparkly pink tee shirt over a pair of torn jeans and grubby flip-flops.

"Oh, hi, Zack. I've finally figured out what I'm going to call this. 'Baby Dear.' It's a play on words, get it? 'Dear' and 'deer'?"

"Yeah, great, that'll work," he said. "This is Madeline Maclin. She's investigating the robbery at the museum."

"Are you related to Cecille?" Phoebe asked.

"My mother," I said.

"Ms. Maclin's painting was stolen," Zack said. "She wants to know if we're the masterminds behind the crime."

Phoebe took him seriously. "Oh, no. I'd never do anything like that, no matter how angry I was."

She didn't look like someone with anger issues. "Were you angry?" I asked.

"Yes, at first. You'd think with my mother on the museum board, I'd have a free pass, but no, they voted to just have paintings. Now I'm glad I didn't have anything there, although my work is much more difficult for a thief to carry off."

She gestured toward her work, jumbles of unrelated objects tangled together with chicken wire, duct tape, and extension cords. I could see some beauty and form in Zack's work, but Phoebe's looked like a junkyard had exploded in her back yard.

"Do the police have any suspects?" she asked.

"They haven't said. But they think it was an inside job."

"My mother will be thrilled about that." She reached into the pocket of her jeans and took out a piece of colored wire which she twisted idly around her finger. "I wish there was something we could do to help you out."

"You can keep your ears and eyes open for any lead on the missing paintings," I said. "If you're not familiar with them, you can see them on the museum's website. If you hear anything at all, please call me." We exchanged phone numbers, and I admired a few more of Phoebe's tangles before Zack and I walked back to his studio.

He put his gloves on and slid his glasses back in place. "Sorry I sounded so insensitive. I hope you find your painting."

"I know what it's like to be overlooked. You had every right to be upset."

"Even if I wanted to take the paintings, I don't know how to get into the museum after hours and neither does Phoebe."

"Even though your mother is director and Phoebe's in on the museum board?"

"We both have mother issues."

I hear you, I wanted to say.

Zack turned the stone around on his work bench. "The times I was there, security was tight. Maybe the thief is somebody who works at the museum."

"Why would a museum employee steal paintings?"

"Maybe he or she needed the money."

"Where would they sell stolen artwork?"

He shrugged. "I have no idea."

CHAPTER FIVE

I sent Jerry a text to let him know I was on my way to Pot Luck Alley. He was waiting in front of Del's pawn shop, but didn't have any news on the paintings.

"Del says he'll be on the lookout," he said. "How about you? Any luck?"

I handed him my lists and carefully drove the car down the narrow alley. "Letticia Booth, museum director, hired me to solve this mystery, but there's a lot more mystery than we first thought. Several odd things have happened in the past month, and all of them make Letticia look incompetent. Failing to meet a grant deadline, a fake painting, a missing shipment, and now the gala robbery."

"She must be feeling pretty paranoid."

"Oh, here's the most interesting part. Someone left a note on her desk that says, 'Ignore the real artist and this museum gets what it deserves.'"

"So who's this real artist?"

"Mystery number one."

"And the museum will get what it deserves? That doesn't make a lot of sense. Taking down a museum? That doesn't sound like an exciting life goal to me."

"Or me." I indicated the lists. "I talked with Doug and Dawn Elmore who helped write the grant. Dawn said she left it on Letticia's desk and that's the last anyone saw of it."

"The grant people won't let the museum resubmit their proposal?"

"According to Dawn, the Hester Fulton Memorial Museum Grants and Bequests is apparently far too stuffy and rigid to allow that."

"Hester," Jerry said thoughtfully. "Hester Fairweather."

Jerry was constantly making up names for the imaginary child we might have one day, and I was constantly shooting them down. "No."

"Has a nice sort of wind-blown quality, don't you think?" He wiggled his fingers in the air. "Hester Fairweather."

"Again, no," I said. "I also spoke with Zack Turner, who happens to be Letticia Booth's son. He's peeved because his mom won't let him show his work in the museum. He's also overly sensitive about his sculptures. We visited his next door neighbor, Phoebe, Roxanna Deluca's daughter. She's in her own little art world of twisted wire."

"Two people who consider themselves real artists."

"Yes, indeed."

"What about Jake? Did he shadow you all day?"

"Just most of the morning before his boss called him away to track Elvis. He's very excited to be part of my investigation."

"You will find he's excited about everything."

When we got home, I realized I hadn't stopped for lunch and was amazingly hungry. While Jerry fixed something for us to eat, I read over my list of artists. Maybe one of them had a rival. Maybe one of them stole their own painting to throw suspicion on a rival. Then there was the access problem. Was there a night time cleaning crew? Letticia Booth hadn't mentioned a cleaning crew, but wouldn't they be in the gallery, vacuuming and dusting for the gala?

By the time Jerry brought a ham and cheese sandwich on crusty bread and a big glass of milk, my head was spinning. He set the food on the little table between the rocking chairs. "Got it figured out?"

"I've already talked to six of the docents. So that's ten more and possibly a night crew. I might as well resign myself to a lot of talking."

I'd almost finished my sandwich when we heard the familiar roar of Austin Terrell's four-wheeler.

"I'd better make some more sandwiches," Jerry said.

Austin, a sturdy ten year old white boy, and his friend Denisha Simpson, a confident little black girl, stopped by almost every day to see what we were doing and what we were having for dinner. Austin's newest toy was a bright red four-wheeler. He arrived in a spray of gravel. He took off his helmet, and his spiky hair sprang to attention.

"Jerry! I found another haunted house for us to explore."

"Great. Where is it?"

"Down near Bylow's farm. You know where that is? The old man Tumpty used to live there."

"Did you call him old man Humpty Tumpty?"

Austin stared. "How did you know?"

"Where's Denisha?" I asked.

"She's coming. It takes longer on her bike. I told her she could ride on the back of my four-wheeler. I got an extra helmet, but she says it's too dangerous, even though I told her it's a Polaris 570, and two people can ride on it. She's way too cautious."

I could see Denisha coming across the field. "There she is."

Austin had more to say about the haunted house. "Somebody told me that you can see blood running down the walls, and there's this really bad smell in the basement like maybe zombies live down there."

"Sounds cool," Jerry said. "We'll check it out, but not today."

"That's okay. Anytime works for me. What are you eating, Madeline? That looks good."

"Come on in the kitchen," Jerry said. "I'll fix you one."

Denisha arrived on her bike, looking calm and collected, as usual. She parked the bike under a tree and came up onto the porch.

"Good afternoon, Madeline."

"Hello, Denisha. How was your day?"

She sat down in a rocking chair. "Very nice, thank you. You are going to be the first to hear my big news. I've decided to open my own detective agency."

"That's very good news."

"I thought if you ever got really busy and needed to send some clients to me, I'd be happy to help you out."

"I will definitely keep you in mind."

"Actually, I may have a client very soon. My aunt has lost her charm bracelet, and I told her I'd find it. So my first case is going to be the *Mystery of the Missing Charm Bracelet*. I thought I'd write it all down, too, and maybe Shana could help me get it published."

"I'm sure she'd be glad to help you."

Denisha gave me a thoughtful look with her big brown eyes. "Hayden's mother died, did you know? And his pet ferret. It's made him really sad, and he's wandering off. You need to be on the lookout for him."

"Yes, he's going through a rough time right now."

"I'm not sure what I'd do if my aunt died."

"There would be lots of people to look out for you."

She thought this over and abruptly changed the subject. "Are you doing anything for the SkinkFest this year?"

The SkinkFest was Celosia's annual fall festival honoring the small striped lizards that skittered over walls and porches, losing their blue tails to cats and dogs all over town. When I asked someone why a skink fest, they replied that everything else had been taken. Jerry and I had been out of town last year and missed the celebration. "I don't think so."

"We ought to have a booth to advertise our detective agencies."

Austin returned to the porch in time to hear this. He spoke through a mouthful of sandwich. "What's that got to do with skinks?"

"Not everything has to be about skinks."

"Yes, it does. Why do you think they call it a SkinkFest? Are you solving mysteries about lizards?"

Before they came to blows, I said, "That's a good idea, Denisha, but I believe it costs a lot of money to have a booth on Main Street."

She'd already thought of this. "If we start saving now, we'd have enough by next month."

"The Mystery of the Missing Tails!" Austin enjoyed his joke so much he almost choked on his sandwich.

Denisha rolled her eyes at me as Jerry pounded Austin on the back. "See what being silly gets you?"

He caught his breath. "It was a good joke. Admit it."

"How about dessert?" Jerry asked, successfully diverting the conversation. The kids were happy with chocolate chip cookies, and skinks were forgotten.

***

Jake, however, hadn't forgotten me or *From Crown to Crime*. Soon after Austin and Denisha headed for home, the purple Gremlin chugged up the drive, and Jake hopped out, phone in hand. His shirt was a tame yellow, but his tie was a bright pattern of orange and red flames.

He took the porch steps two at a time. "Got a preview for you, Madeline. You're gonna love it. Hey, are those chocolate chip?"

Jerry handed him the bag. "I think the kids left a few."

"Thanks. Great tie."

Jerry had on a green tie with large bunches of purple grapes. "In honor of *Flower of the South*."

"Oh, yeah, believe me, I heard all about the dueling dramas this morning."

"Your tie is pretty spectacular."

"Madeline and I are on fire to solve this mystery. Gotta go with the theme." He pulled up a rocking chair, and after gulping down a couple of cookies, turned his phone so we could see the screen. "Premiere episode of *From Crown to Crime*!"

I was curious to see what Jake had done with the video and was pleased with the result. He had edited the scenes in my office, and I looked reasonably calm and confident. The scenes in the house showcased my artwork.

Jake's expression was hopeful. "Everything's good, right? Now, what we really need is a good intro, you in full pageant regalia, crown and everything, saying something like, 'I used to be a beauty queen until I realized my true calling.' Then we'll cut to you in your office, looking all professional, and you say, "Now I solve mysteries and fight crime!'"

I took a long moment to consider Jake's concept. What he said was exactly true. I used to be a beauty queen until I realized my true calling. Now I did solve mysteries and, in a way, fought crime. The question was did I want this spread across the internet?

Well, why not? Nothing about my life was a secret. Maybe I could inspire little girls and young women to be whatever they wanted to be. No one had to be only one thing in life.

"What do you think, Madeline?"

"I'll have control over the content, of course."

"Of course!"

I caught Jerry's eye, and he grinned. "I think it's cool."

I turned to Jake with a smile. "Let's do it." He sat back in his chair, relieved. "I kept some of my short pageant dresses for special occasions, but my mother has all my crowns and tiaras."

"No problem!" Jake said. "I got one in the car."

"You travel with a tiara?" Jerry asked.

"I knew Madeline would agree, so I borrowed one from the *Galaxy* storeroom. You wouldn't believe the stuff we've got back there."

I showed Jake the dresses, and he chose a silver and gold number with lots of bugle beads. It wasn't a gown, but he said I'd be sitting down for the intro, so that didn't matter. I wrangled my dark curls into a more proper style and fixed the *Galaxy* tiara on top. Then I put on full makeup, including eyelashes and mascara and a deep rose-colored lipstick. It had been a long time since I'd gone full-out pageant, so I hardly recognized myself, but Jake and Jerry assured me I looked fantastic. We decided the best backdrop for all this glamour was the living room. I sat down on the sofa, put on my best pageant smile, and gave my best pageant wave to the camera.

"Hello, everyone, and welcome to my YouTube channel. My name is Madeline Maclin, your former Miss Parkland. I used to be a beauty queen until I realized my true calling."

I recorded this several times until Jake and I were happy with the results. "We'll record the second part tomorrow at your office," he said. "Really glad you're going along with this, Madeline."

I handed him the tiara. "Time to get back to the real me."

"Oh, keep it. We might need it for some future shots. This is amazing stuff. We're looking at millions of subscribers."

I grinned at Jake's never-ending enthusiasm for this project. "I hope so."

"Now as much as I'd like to hang around , I got a lead on a UFO sighting I'd better check out, or Basil will have me back in the sewers looking for mole people. As much as I like wandering through the sewers, I've done enough of that in my day. Catch ya tomorrow?"

"I'll be in my office at nine," I said.

"See ya then."

As Jake hurried out to his car, Jerry put both arms around my waist. "Miss Parkland doesn't have to change clothes unless she really wants to."

My kiss left a big rose-colored mark on his mouth. "Miss Parkland is dying to get out of this dress."

"Let me help you."

Jerry was unzipping my dress when my phone rang. The caller ID said "Winthrope Worthingham."

"I'd better get that," I said. "Mr. Worthingham is one of the local artists on my list."

Winthrope Worthingham, despite his fancy name, had a thick Southern accent. "Miz Maclin? Doug Elmore tells me you was investigatin' the theft of our artwork."

"That's right," I said. "I believe your painting is *Musings on McDonald's?*" *Musings on McDonald's* was the mass of red and yellow swirls, exploding ketchup and mustard packets, I assumed.

"Yes, ma'am, and I wanna tell you right now not to worry about it. It was a print. I got the original here at my house. Hope I can count on your discretion. Wasn't sure how the museum might feel about it being only a print."

"I think the museum will be relieved the thief didn't get your original," I said. "I still plan to find the paintings. Would you want your print back?"

"Nah, that's okay," he said. "Appreciate you lookin' for the others, though. They can't all be prints."

No, they can't. "Mr. Worthingham, did the museum invite you to participate in the gala, or did you ask to be included?"

"The museum asked me to send something in and I did. It was

right nice of them, but I didn't go round shouting out the news, if that's what you mean. Just said thanks and sent in *Musings.*"

"All right, Mr. Worthingham. Thank you."

I ended the call. "I can check Winthrope off my artist list. His ode to fast food wasn't his original painting and he didn't want to advertize it."

"So who's next on that list?"Jerry asked.

"Tully Springfield."

"He didn't send one of his clown paintings, did he? I'd hate to think of that looming over the hors d'oeuvres."

"He actually sent two of his landscapes." Jerry and I had met Tully Springfield when I was investigating the murder of Juliet Lovelace, my first case in Celosia. He lived way out on Highway 12 near the Virginia border surrounded by some of the most garish yard art I'd ever seen. Tully's landscapes of the mountains were stunning, but he dismissed them in favor of truly horrible clown paintings.

"So are we headed that way tomorrow?"

"As I recall, Tully doesn't have a phone. We'll have to."

"I wonder how many clown pictures he's done since our last visit."

"I'm not sure I want to subject even our imaginary unborn child to that. Okay, where were we?"

"About halfway down."

I'd slithered out of the dress and had my arms around Jerry when my phone buzzed again. I checked the ID. "It's Mom." I took a deep breath and answered as cheerfully as possible. "Hello, Mom, how are you?"

"Letticia says she hired you to find out what happened. Have you found out anything?"

There was no escaping Mom's network. "I talked to several people at the museum today, and I'm going to follow a lead to-morrow."

"You need to work as fast as you can, Madeline. I can't take the stress."

"I'll do my best. Oh, and Mom, do you still have your key to the museum?"

"It should be in my pocketbook. Why?"
"Will you check, please?"
After a few minutes, she said, "Yes, I still have it."
We said good-by, and Jerry gave me an amused look.
"Clowns or your mother. It's a tough call."
I leaned in for a serious kiss. "No more calls."

CHAPTER SIX

Thursday morning at nine Jake was right on time. His shirt and tie gleamed in jarring neon green and orange. The tie had a pattern of bug-eyed goldfish. He parked himself in the client chair and took out his phone.

"Good morning, Madeline. All set for another exciting day in the life of Miss Private Eye?"

"I'm ready," I said. "What's the latest on your UFO?"

"You are not going to believe this, but North Carolina is a hotbed of UFO activity. Lots of sightings recently, but to tell you the truth, I'm still real gung-ho about *From Crown to Crime*. If only there was something more exciting going on. My boss says the set-up is okay, but the plot's too tame. He's really pushing me to find something more gripping."

"Break-ins and thefts aren't awful enough for him?"

"This is the *Galaxy* we're talking about. There's no such thing as awful enough."

"The car chase comes at the end."

He chuckled. "Yeah, I hope so. What've you got going on to-day?"

"More people to talk to."

"Let's go ahead and record the rest of the intro." Jake surveyed the items on my desk. "Too bad you don't have a big magnifying glass. Guess that's too cliché. A blood-stained clue would be great. You don't carry a gun, do you? I should have thought to bring one."

"No guns."

He decided my laptop, a stack of notes, and a serious look from me would be enough for a start. He aimed the phone my way. "Okay, intro, take one."

I didn't have a problem speaking to the little phone. After all, I'd faced numerous panels of judges. I pretended one had asked, "Here's your question, Miss Greater Woodlawn Area. As a private investigator, what would you say have been your greatest successes?"

I didn't call upon my pageant smile for my answer. I looked as serious as I could. "Now I solve mysteries and fight crime. I've solved five murders in Celosia, including murder at the Miss Celosia Pageant, the death of movie director Josh Gaskins, the murders of Amelia Lever and Wendall Clarke, and most recently, I discovered who killed the young man at Phoenix Vineyard. Now I'm on another case involving the theft of valuable art work from the Parkland Museum of Art."

Jake paused the recording. "That's great! Now we need something like, 'Follow me as I show you how my beauty queen experience prepared me for this fascinating and difficult job.' Unless there's something else you'd like to say."

Since my beauty queen experience had in an odd way prepared me, I agreed, and recorded this, too.

Jake was pleased with the result. "We don't need another take. You sounded like a real professional there. I'll edit this with the first part, and we're good to go." He paused for a moment, his bright blue eyes serious. "Thanks, Madeline. You see, as much as I love snooping around in the paranormal, I think a story like yours will really resonate with people. Plus your show could be my ticket out of the tabloids. If *From Crown to Crime* is a hit, I'm one step closer, but I gotta convince my boss this show is worth pursuing." His serious moment was over, and he grinned. "So, these people you need to talk to. Any way I can help?"

Jake wasn't on the case, but while he was following me around, I might as well give him something useful to do. Besides Tully and Winthrope Worthingham there were six more artists on my list. And then there was the other list, the one with all the special guests, the patrons of the arts. Maybe the easiest way to handle this was through the *Galaxy's* resources.

I showed Jake that list. "How difficult would it be for you to search the *Galaxy* database for any stories involving these people?"

"It would be a snap," he said. "What are we looking for?"

"I was thinking more along the lines of financial problems, connections to the museum, that sort of thing."

"Pageant connections?"

"Sure. Why not?"

"I'm on it." He started for the door and turned. "Oh, one more thing. Is it okay if I call your mother and get some pageant back story on you for the channel?"

I had no idea how my mother would react to a reporter from the *Galaxy*, but as long as he asked about pageants, she would probably be agreeable. "You'd better let me be there when you talk to her."

"Yeah, sure. Hey, you think she'd like to be on YouTube?"

In her present state, no. "You can ask her."

"Check with you later," he said and dashed out.

***

I decided to start my day with museum board member, Roxanna Deluca, Phoebe's mother. She agreed to meet me at the museum coffee shop. She swept through the coffee shop as if she owned it and sat down at my table. She was tall and thin with a distinctive nose. Her long fingernails were painted black to match her black dress and long black hair, which she swept back with a toss of her head.

"You must be Madeline. You don't look at all like your mother."

And in complete contrast to you, your daughter looks like a fairy princess, I wanted to say. "Thank you for coming, Mrs. Deluca."

"Roxanna, please." She snapped her fingers at the waiter. "Two coffees, black," she ordered without asking my preference. She turned back to me. "Letticia tells me you're investigating the break-in. What's the latest?"

"I'm interviewing anyone connected with the museum and the gala. The artists, employees, patrons, and board members. Can you tell me if you've noticed anything unusual regarding the gala?"

"Hmm." She sat back in her chair and rubbed her chin. I could almost hear the witch purring, "Ahh, poppies."

"I'd have to think about that."

"Is it true that Zack Turner was supposed to participate in the gala?"

"No. He was never really considered. He's Letticia's son, so sorry, boy, you're out."

"What about your daughter?"

This set her off. "Oh, my lord, what she calls art is ridiculous. Anyone could go to the dump, scoop up a pile of trash, and put it on display. She knows we can't have that kind of rubbish in the gallery. I told her she could move to that little artsy town and get this out of her system. She felt slighted, but she'd never act on that feeling. If you're thinking she took offense and masterminded this robbery, then think again. Phoebe has all the initiative of a sloth."

And I thought my mother was rough.

Our coffees arrived. I thanked the waiter.

Roxanna didn't even look at him. She gave her coffee a brief stir and a tentative sip. "Ugh, I see the coffee hasn't improved. You've spoken with the artists?"

"Yes, and with several of the volunteers."

"You think they were involved? Most of them are too feeble to lift a painting off the wall."

"Someone could've let the thief or thieves in."

"True. But why? This was to be a fund raiser for the museum. The paintings were good, but they weren't by Renoir. Why target a little gala?"

"That's what I'm trying to find out. Do you still have a key to the museum?"

She gave me a sharp look. "Yes. I usually come in early to work on displays. Why do you ask?

"Someone could have taken your key."

She took her black purse and thunked it onto the table. She

pulled out a key and held it up as if to say, how dare you accuse me of losing this?

"Thank you," I said.

She shoved the key back into her purse and took another sip of her coffee. She grimaced and set her cup down. "Why did you decide to become a detective?"

From Crown to Crime, take two. "I like the challenge of finding things, solving mysteries."

"Doesn't sound like something I'd enjoy. Now isn't your husband involved with some sort of criminal element? Your mother said something about this."

Thanks, Mom.

"Have you asked him about this break-in? He might know who's behind it."

"He's helping me with my investigation."

She took one more sip. "I'm not paying for this. Excuse me."

I thanked her for her time and left her at the register, berating the wait staff for their inferior coffee.

***

I had a call from Jake that his search was underway. "One of the secretaries owes me a favor, so I got her digging up the dirt on those names you gave me," he said. "Is it okay if I call your mom now?"

"Yes, I'm on my way to see her." I called Mom to let her know I was in town, and I'd stop by with a report if that was convenient.

"Now would be a good time," she said.

She looked perfectly groomed from her black heels to her tailored black skirt and crisp white blouse. Her favorite pearl earrings dangled from her ears, and she had on three jeweled bracelets and a silver wrist watch. I thought she might still be upset, but there was a gleam in her eye.

"Madeline, I had a phone call from someone who said he was doing a television program about you. Is this true?"

"It's in the planning stages."

"It sounds wonderful. He's interested in your pageant experiences, and I told him I had all your pictures and trophies. He should be here in the next few minutes."

"The main emphasis will be on my investigations."

"Oh, of course, that, too." We sat down in the living room. Mom rearranged the centerpiece on the coffee table a fraction of an inch. "I was relieved to hear Letticia hired you. Goodness knows she can afford it. You know her family is very wealthy. Her father was Edmund Booth of the Archville Booths. At one time they owned half the town, and they have an amazing mansion on Larger Lake. I've been there several times for dinner. It all belongs to Letticia now. I hope she'll keep it up the way her parents did."

Rattling on about her social contacts seemed to calm her, so I let her tell me all about the Parkland scene until Jake arrived. His grin and his charm were on full blast, and he knew exactly what to say.

"Mrs. Maclin, it's a pleasure to meet you. Thanks for seeing me during what must be a difficult time for you. I promise I won't take much of your time, but I want to know all about Madeline's pageant life."

"Come in, come in," she said. "The display case is right over here."

She led Jake to a separate parlor where she kept every pho-to, ribbon, program, and tiara in two large glass fronted cabinets. "Here's Madeline in her very first pageant, Little Miss Parkland. She came in second, which was not what I'd hoped, but she did very well considering."

I barely remembered Little Miss Parkland, since I'd been five and not sure what all the fuss was about.

Mom went down the line. "Here's where she won Miss Living Doll, Miss Sweet and Sassy, and Junior Miss Guilford County."

The list rolled on. Jake made admiring comments and took pictures and videos.

"And this is you playing the violin, Madeline?"

I sighed inwardly. "Yes. 'Orange Blossom Special,' my one and only piece."

"Always a show stopper," Mom said.

"Might make a great theme song for the show," Jake said.

"I don't play anymore."

"Oh, but you could take it up again," Mom said.

"I'm a little busy with other things."

After Jake had seen every possible pageant memento, Mom offered him tea, and we returned to the living room.

She fixed Jake with her sternest gaze. "Now, Mr. Banner, I do have a concern. The *Galaxy* is not a reputable paper."

"No, ma'am, but this program will be. My goal is to find a real story, an important story, so I can leave the tabloids. I don't mind telling you my wife is encouraging me to do just that. You may know her family. She's Christine Snowden."

Mom looked pleasantly surprised. "I knew her father. Does she still have that beautiful country home?"

"Yes, she does. Snowden Manor. I'm happy to say I live there now. You don't have a thing to worry about, Mrs. Maclin. *From Crown to Crime* is going to be a quality production."

"*From Crown to Crime*? Is that what you're calling the program?"

"Oh, it's not going to be just one program about the muse-um break-in. I'm planning to make it a series. Madeline's solved enough mysteries to keep this going a long time."

Mention of the break-in brought back my mother's gloomy outlook. "I hope she can. I'm counting on her to save my reputa-tion. You can't imagine what I've been through. I'm practically a prisoner in my own house."

"Mom, you can go out," I said. "The police asked you to stay in town, that's all."

"You know I can't stand the idea of people talking about me behind my back."

"I don't think they are."

"How do you know? You have no idea about the type of wom-en I deal with. I'm sure they are eating up every little scrap of bad news about me."

Jake set his tea glass on the table, being careful, I noticed, to use the coaster. "Well, I've got everything I need, ladies, so if you'll excuse me."

Mom thanked him for coming, and I saw him out.

"All right," he said. "I got some useful stuff here. Still kinda tame. But it's all part of the process. I get it. We'll let your audience see how this evolves, the gritty day to day, piece by piece investigation technique, cornering suspects and digging out their secrets. It'll be a good contrast to the actual solving of the crime, which oughta be big and splashy, right?"

"Right," I said.

"Who are we talking to next?"

"An artist named Tully Springfield. I'll send you his address."

Jake bounded down the walk. "See ya there!"

Mom came up behind me in time to see Jake take off in his purple Gremlin.

"What a bizarre little man, Madeline. But he has excellent connections."

CHAPTER SEVEN

Jerry had finished his shift at Deely's, so we headed out to Tully Springfield's. I remembered the split rail fence, each rail a different color, and the fish-shaped mailbox painted to resemble Uncle Sam, complete with top hat. The yard art was still a psychedelic wonderland of frogs, deer, wagon wheels, and birdbaths, all painted in Day-Glo colors and wild patterns. Every inch of the house was covered in smiling faces, butterflies, and climbing cats. Tully still had Jerry's uncle's 57 Chevy, which he had adorned in paisley patterns.

Jake's purple Gremlin fit right in. He hopped out of his car and started taking pictures. "This place is amazing."

"Hello!" Tully's voice called. "I'm around back."

We circled more art to the back of the house with its splendid view of the Blue Ridge Mountains. Tully appeared the same, a youthful-looking man with gray hair and blue eyes. He wore faded jeans and a shirt streaked with paint.

"Madeline! Jerry! Nice to see you."

"This is Jake Banner," I said, and the two men shook hands.

"Great place you got here," Jake said.

"Thanks. I was just finishing this painting. Let me put in one more tree."

The landscape, like all of Tully's non-clown work, was an amazing creation of light and shadow that captured the grandeur and mystery of the distant hills.

I took a closer look. "How do you get those clouds to look so real?"

"Oh, I turn my brush like so, and then I give it a little flick. Nothing to it. What brings you out this way?"

Nothing to it. I planned to practice that move as soon as I got back to my studio. "I wanted to talk to you about the break-in at the museum. I'm really sorry your paintings were taken." I checked my list. "*Mountain Vista* and *Mountain Vista 2*?"

He stopped in mid-tree. "Madeline, I wouldn't worry about that. Thank goodness I only sent in landscapes. Imagine if I'd sent in one of my clown portraits. It would have been so much worse if that was stolen." He brightened. "Oh, but you haven't seen my latest collection. I call it *Last Circus*."

Jerry grinned at me, but thankfully didn't say anything. Tully led the way into the huge studio that overlooked those glorious mountains. I braced myself, but no amount of bracing was enough for the onslaught of *Last Circus*. Tully showed us a large selection of clowns, only these were all crying multicolored tears. In the background, sad-eyed children watched as circus tents sagged and circus wagons rolled off into the sunset.

All I could think of was *Thank God they're going away*. "I don't know what to say, Tully."

"I know. It's too emotional. When I was working on the collection, I had such mixed feelings. Was it too sad? Was it too strong for the viewing public? Would it be too intense for small children? But everything turned out the way I wanted it to."

"I'm overcome," Jerry said.

"It affects everyone that way."

Jake asked if he could take a few photos, but Tully said the collection wasn't ready.

"Not sure this stuff would ever be ready," Jake said in an undertone to me. "I've seen some creepy things in my line of work, and I'm adding this to my top ten list."

"Thank God I didn't send any of these to the gala," Tully said again. "I would have been devastated."

I turned so I was facing him and not the nightmare that was *Last Circus*. "What's your take on the theft of the paintings?"

"You know I don't get the newspaper, and my TV reception up

here is poor at best. I wish I could help you, but I have no idea."

"Okay. Letticia Booth said you discovered that one of their paintings was a forgery."

"Oh, yes," he said. "*Yellow Sky Number 13* by Raymond Halsey."

"How did you know it was a fake?"

"I studied with Halsey years ago, back when his work was more representational. Now he does these peculiar modern art paintings. But I recognized some of his signature brush work had been forced."

"And no one at the museum noticed this?"

"Well, it was an extremely slight difference." He moved one of the clown paintings over to one side. "I felt so sorry for Letticia. I understand she took the blame. I don't think I would have even looked at the painting if Roxanna hadn't showed it to me. I don't care for modern art."

"Roxanna Deluca wanted you to see it?"

Not satisfied with the effect, he moved the painting back to its original spot. "That's better. All the board members wanted me to see it. They were so proud to have a genuine Halsey. I sincerely hated telling them it was not genuine."

Tully invited us to stay longer, but we declined. He also tried to give us a birdbath, but we reminded him we already had one from our last visit, one of the more subtle ones. Jake thanked him for the offer but said he'd pass. By the time we made our way back to our cars, Tully had already drifted back to his landscape.

"That is one flaky guy," Jake said. "Can't see him making the effort to steal anything. What's next?"

"Jerry and I are going home to regroup," I said.

"Okay, I'll go see how things are progressing with the dirt list. I'll have some footage for you to preview tomorrow. I'll text you when it's ready. This is gonna be good."

Off he went. Jerry and I enjoyed the silence for a few moments.

"How about some dinner?" Jerry said. "We passed an interesting little place a few miles before Tully's."

The little place was called Betty Lou's, and it advertised "Country Cookin'." We sat down at one of the small wooden tables and checked out the menus.

"You know it's good if the g's missing," Jerry said. "Look, all the g's are missing. Or should I say, missin.' I want corn bread and turnip greens with all the fixin's."

"I'll have the chicken and gravy, roastin' all day."

The waitress greeted us and took our order. "Be right back with your drinks," she said.

"As absent minded as Tully is, I'm a little surprised he remembered to take his mountain paintings to the museum," I said. "I can't see him having anything to do with the robbery."

"Me, either," Jerry said."

"Speaking of absent minded, have you heard from Hayden today?"

Jerry took out his phone. "I'll give him a call." He let the phone ring for a few moments and started to end the call when Hayden answered. "Hey, buddy, what's up?" He listened, his expression concerned. "Yeah, we're on our way back. I'm sure we can find it. Okay, here she is." He handed his phone to me.

Hayden's voice was on the edge of panic. "Madeline, I can't find my green notebook. I have to find it. It has all the notes for my song cycle. It's my only copy. I don't know what I was thinking having only one copy. I have to find it."

"Where are you?" I asked. "Is Shana with you?"

"Shana's in Parkland recording an interview with one of the local TV stations, and I can't reach her. I'm at home. I've turned my office upside down, and my notebook isn't here!"

"Did you take it somewhere else? Have you been working on the porch, or in the living room?" A long pause made me wonder if he'd passed out from anxiety. "Hayden?"

"Give me your phone," Jerry said. "I'll call Shana."

Hayden's voice came back. "I'm in the bedroom. I forgot I was working in my notebook last night."

"Do you see it?"

Another long pause. Shana must have finished her interview because she answered the phone. "Shana," Jerry said, "Hayden's freaking out over his green notebook. Any idea where it might be? Yeah, he's looking in the bedroom. He's on my phone with Mac.

She's trying to talk him down off the ledge."

"Here it is!" Hayden's shout made me jump. "Thank God!"

"He's found it," Jerry told Shana. "Are you on your way home? That's a good idea."

I heard Hayden take some deep breaths. "It had fallen between the bed and the nightstand."

"Why don't you lie down on the bed since you're right there?" I said. "Shana's on her way home. After you rest a little, make a copy of your poems."

"I will, thank you. And thank Jerry for me."

Hayden assured me he was all right, so I ended the call, and Jerry and I exchanged phones.

"I'm glad you're not a sensitive artist," Jerry said. "Wait, that didn't sound right. Overly sensitive, I should've said."

"Well, on top of everything, Hayden is dealing with depression. It's a good thing he's staying with us while Shana's out of town."

The waitress brought our drinks and our food, which didn't need those extra g's to be delicious. Shana called to report that she was home, and Hayden was okay.

"But I told him he absolutely has to stay with you while I'm on tour. He has a doctor's appointment tomorrow. We're hoping a change of medicine will help. Of course, an acceptance letter from his publisher would really help."

I was glad to hear he was all right. "Tell him he can move in any time."

***

Letticia had given me the phone number for Specialty Transport, the company that handled playground equipment. On our way home, I called the company and spoke to the secretary who handled orders.

"We did have an order of equipment for the Parkland Museum," he said. "Let me see. Hold on a minute. Here it is. Yes, the next day, someone called and canceled the order. It wasn't a problem. Things like this happen all the time."

"Do you know who called you?"

"No, I'm sorry. It was someone from the museum, a woman, if that helps."

"And the call itself was from the museum?"

"Yes, the same phone number."

I thanked him and ended the call. "The secretary says a woman called from the museum and canceled the order. That does not narrow things down very much."

"It could have been a mistake," Jerry said. "Maybe this person misunderstood and thought Letticia wanted the order canceled."

"Maybe," I said. "The fellow at Specialty Transport wasn't concerned about the cancelation. It really is a small thing compared to missing a grant deadline or buying a fake painting, but if you add up all these incidents, it looks like Letticia's position is on very shaky ground."

"This is sounding more and more like a con job," Jerry said. "Do you want me to look into this?

Such a loaded question. I wanted Jerry out of the game. He was doing his best to stay out, and yet, we always circled back to his alternate universe and the people who lived in it. "We already have Sobbin' Susie and her mystery con," I said. "You know how I feel about that."

"Some discreet inquiries?"

"Let me think about it."

***

At home, I sent Jake a text to ask if he'd uncovered anything about the people who were invited to the gala.

"I've never seen a bunch of people so squeaky clean," was his reply. "A couple of parking tickets, that's all. I'll keep looking."

I was able to reach two more artists on my list. One wasn't too upset as he had already sent in an insurance claim. The other, who had the two portraits in the gala titled *Grandpa Ellis* and *Granma Ann*, was very upset and didn't want to talk to me. That left Anastacia Symphony, whose watercolor, *Symphony in Pastels*, resembled a child's chalk drawing that had been left out in the rain, an artist who went by the name of Trigger Fish, who'd painted a seascape called *Crystal Coast*, and Wallace Everly, whose dramatic oil painting, *Fire on the Mountain*, was a strikingly affecting representation of a forest fire, tendrils of smoke reaching up past starkly outlined trees surrounding a shadowy mountain. No one could think of anyone who might have been slighted, or who felt they had been ignored.

"Anastacia Symphony Fairweather," Jerry said when I told him. "There's a name that sings. But, oh, my god, Trigger Fish."

"No," I said.

"Trigger Fish Fairweather. Please. That's fantastic."

I tried to say it and got tongue-tied, which made Jerry laugh even harder.

Shana called to say she and Hayden were on their way. When they arrived, Jerry told Hayden he could park his blue and white Mini Cooper beside his red Jeep. I showed Hayden the available upstairs bedrooms. He took the bedroom overlooking the front yard. He set his suitcase by the bed. "I can't thank you enough for letting me stay. I'm always a little uneasy when Shana's gone."

"No need to stay by yourself unless you want to. You have your own bathroom down the hall, and I'll get you a key to the front door."

Shana left me all the important phone numbers, gave Hayden a good-by kiss and final instructions, and drove off in her car. The guys entertained themselves with a video game while I worked in my studio. I say I worked, but really I stared out the window as Uncle Val's little bats danced in the darkening sky. Unlike my other cases, there wasn't a body. No one had been murdered. But this theft was a serious blow to me and my fellow artists and could be the death of Letticia Booth's career. I was not going to let that happen.

CHAPTER EIGHT

Friday morning, I was awakened by thunderous strains of music. Jerry's parents and his older sister had been opera buffs, and that's all he heard during his early years. He tended to go for the lesser known operas, like *Paul Bunyan* and *The Ballad of Baby Doe*, but even I knew this was Wagner blasting out of the speakers.

I staggered downstairs to the kitchen where Jerry handed me my essential large cup of coffee. I pulled out a chair and sat down at the table. "That's a little intense for this time of day, isn't it?" I asked.

Jerry plopped two pieces of bread into the toaster. "We need inspiration."

"We have a guest who might like to sleep in."

"Oh, I checked on Hayden. He's sound asleep. Those new pills of his must be working."

"Any reason you're going with Wagner this morning?"

"I have a plan."

"Jerry."

"Hear me out." He sat down at the table. "I told you the absolute truth about Susie not needing my help with her con. Not now, anyway."

"But you may have to get involved later."

"Yes. *May* have to get involved. Keep that in mind."

I took a big drink of coffee. "Keep going."

"She might be able to help us."

"How and why?"

The toast popped up, so I had to wait until Jerry retrieved it and brought it back to the table. "She came into Big Mike's organization a couple of years after I did, so she has different contacts. As to why, well, we're friends. I'm sure she'd be happy to help out."

I munched on a piece of toast and tried to make sense of this. It wasn't easy with Wagner blaring in the background and my own concerns crowding into my not quite awake brain. "It can't be anything illegal. It can't be anything where I have to depend on Big Mike to save you. That's too risky."

"What if she just calls around to see if there's anyone who knows anything about the museum break-in and the missing paintings? That's what you've got Jake doing, right?"

"Sort of."

Jerry took out his phone. "What do you say? It's up to you."

I was not happy about it, but I didn't have much to go on with this case, so I agreed. "Can you at least turn Wagner down?"

Jerry turned the music down to a reasonable level and called Susie. As he predicted, she was glad to help and promised to call back as soon as she had any information. Jerry went on to his breakfast shift at Deely's while I sat on the porch and called the remaining museum board members. Besides my mother, the Elmores, and Roxanna Deluca, there were eleven members. Of the eight I managed to contact, four supported Letticia's efforts and were of the opinion that many of the incidents were beyond her control, but the remaining four were very concerned about how the museum was being run.

I had returned to the kitchen to get a refill on my coffee when Hayden came in. He had on a blue shirt and jeans and looked rested.

"How did you sleep?" I asked.

"The best in a long time," he said. "I'd like to think it's all this fresh country air, but I believe my new pills may have something to do with it."

"Whatever works."

"I thought I'd sit out on the porch and see if I can get some writing done."

"You want some coffee? Toast? We've got all kinds of cereal."

"Thanks," he said. "I'll fix something."

I sat out on the porch with him to call the three members left on my list, but no one was home. Around eleven, Jake's purple Gremlin zipped up the driveway and came to a halt behind my Mazda. Jake burst forth, a vision in a garish yellow Hawaiian shirt decorated with Day-Glo pink and orange turtles. His phone was out and recording before his car door slammed shut.

"Here's Madeline Maclin on the job, searching for clues to the missing paintings. What have you got, Madeline?"

I indicated my phone. "Trying to reach the last of the museum board members."

"And?"

"Nothing to report, sorry."

He stopped recording and bounded up the porch steps. "Me, neither. How ya doin'. Hayden? I think my wife has your book. Working on something new?"

"Trying to," Hayden said. "I'm in a slump right now."

"I hear ya, pal. We've all hit a dead end." Jake turned to me. "I was hoping you'd have something, Madeline, so I wouldn't have to investigate this mysterious fire people have been seeing in the old A-1 Sports building downtown. Basil's after me to get the story."

"That's going to be more exciting than following me around today."

"Yeah, well, I have to admit I'm intrigued."

"What kind of mysterious fire?" Hayden asked.

"Lots of multi-colored flames, but nothing gets burned. Spooky, huh?"

"I'm not too keen on spooky," Hayden said. "I'll leave that to the professionals like you."

Jake grinned. "And you can have all the poetry." His phone rang and he answered. "Yeah? Yeah, I'm on my way right now. No, I am not following Ms Maclin. No, there's nothing new happening. Okay, okay, I'll be there." He ended the call. "You see what I'm up against? The *Galaxy* must be fed. Catch ya later."

I was able to reach the last three board members. One was in the concerned camp, and the other two were undecided.

"But I don't like the way things are going," one said.

Neither did I.

But Jerry came home with the good news that Susie knew a fellow named Rusty who agreed to talk to us. We had a quick lunch and hopped in the Jeep.

"And what do we know about this Rusty?" I asked.

"Susie said he'd meet us at Lot Eleven of the Summer Retreat Trailer Park," Jerry said.

***

I thought the meeting spot would be in a dark alley, or maybe an abandoned warehouse. Summer Retreat Trailer Park sounded nice, but it was also abandoned. On rare occasions, a tornado will pop up in North Carolina, and mobile homes, especially the cheap flimsy ones, were nicknamed "tornado magnets." That's exactly what had happened at Summer Retreat. The trailer park was deserted. The few remaining trailers were twisted and crumpled, chunks of yellow insulation and particle board littering the ground. A shiny red Corvette stood out like a bonfire in the middle of the meadow. A huge black man unfolded from the Corvette, his arms covered with dark tattoos. His dark moustache goatee combination circled thin lips. The brim of his cowboy hat rested on the rims of opaque sunglasses that hid his eyes.

"Are you sure about this?" I asked Jerry.

He didn't seem concerned. "It's okay."

We got out of the Jeep. The man stayed where he was. We approached him and Jerry said, "Susie sent me."

The man's voice was a deep rumble. "How they running down at the track?"

"Over Easy to win."

This apparently, was the secret code. The big man gave a nod. "Fairweather. Susie said you needed info. What you want to know?"

"Anything you can tell us about the break-in and robbery at the Parkland Museum of Art."

The man's shoulders were so wide and thick, I was surprised he could cross his arms, but he did. A black python tattoo curled around his right bicep. He tipped up the brim of his hat and raised his sunglasses a few inches to give me a dark squinty-eyed stare. "You ever been in a beauty pageant?"

This was not a question I expected to hear from a giant tattooed con man in a deserted trailer park. "I was Miss Parkland several years ago."

"I thought so!" He offered a hand the size of a shovel. "Pleasure to meet you." We shook hands. "Why are you asking questions about this museum job?"

"Because one of my paintings was stolen, and I intend to get it back."

Rusty turned his squint to Jerry. "How do you two know each other?"

"Miss Parkland's my wife."

Rusty gave a brief chuckle. "Well, whadda you know. So she's not in the game?"

"No," Jerry said. "She's a private investigator, and she's been hired to find the paintings and who stole them."

"I see. Well, some help should be coming along right about now."

The deafening roar of motorcycle engines filled the trailer park, accompanied by a cloud of dust. Five gleaming motorcycles spun in and around the Corvette and came to a halt. The drivers, all women, took off their helmets and shook out their hair.

"Damn it," Rusty said. "All y'all didn't need to come. It's Wallie's problem."

"If it's Wallie's problem, it's our problem," said the tallest of the five. She was a very fit young woman with long black hair tied in a braid. She wore tattered jeans and a midriff-baring tee shirt under her motorcycle jacket.

"All right, then," he said grudgingly. "Madeline and Jerry, this is Helga and her friends, Wallie, Orla, Sissy, and Leeta."

Helga gave me a firm handshake. "Nice to meet you."

As the other women dismounted, I saw the words "Helen's Angels" on the backs of their jackets.

"In honor of my mom," Helga explained. "She started the gang. We're all here on account of Wallie having her picture stolen."

Wallie, who was slight and dressed in a red tee shirt decorated with skulls, dusted her hand on her fringed leather pants before shaking my hand. "It's Wallace, actually, after my grandfather."

"You're Wallace Everly?"

"Yep."

"I've been trying to get in touch with you."

"Yeah, Helga said Rusty was going to talk to someone about a museum robbery, so here I am."

I would not want to be on the receiving end of the smoldering glare Rusty gave Helga, but it didn't concern her in the least.

"I said *you* could come along with Wallie," he said. "You."

"When you said museum, I knew you were talking about the art museum, and that's where Wallie had her picture."

Wallie joined in. "And then I said, a woman left a message on my phone, and this might be the same one."

Helga looked at Rusty as if daring him to challenge her authority. "So we all wanted to come, and I said, let's go."

"All right, all right," he said. "Whatever. I shoulda known you'd all want to be involved.

Wallie turned to me. "Do you know anything about my picture?"

"I wish I had something to tell you," I said, "but I'm still looking. I'd hoped you had an idea. Any enemies? Anybody who'd want to steal your painting?"

"Nope. Ain't got any enemies, and the gang's been real supportive of my art."

The other three women stood by the Corvette. Orla had dark brown skin, coppery curls, and very pale eyes. Twins Sissy and Leeta wore leather vests, torn jeans, and baseball caps to keep their long blond hair in place. Besides their leather jackets, all the women had tattoos, piercings, and many corded and silver bracelets.

"That's right," Orla said. "We would surely like to get our hands on whoever took her artwork. *Fire on the Mountain*'s her best piece yet."

Rusty resigned himself to the fact that the whole gang was now part of the team. "Ladies," he said, "you are looking at a former

Miss Parkland now turned private eye, so anything we can find out is gonna help her find Wallie's picture."

"Miss Parkland, huh?" Helga said. "You still doing pageants?"

"No, I gave that up a long time ago." I said.

"But you know all about them, right?"

"Yes," I said, wondering where this conversation was heading.

She glanced back at the other women who all gave her a nod as if this was a go-ahead signal. "We got a ten year anniversary coming up at Streetwise Designs a week from next Thursday. That's where Rusty and some other guys do custom body work. We wanted to do a promotional deal, something fun to celebrate. Somebody mentioned having a Miss Streetwise Pageant. Not a serious pageant. Something silly for fun. But we could use some pointers. How to walk and stand and all that stuff."

As long as no little girls were involved. "Are all the contestants legally aged women who want to do this?" I asked.

"Oh, yeah, it'll just be us and maybe a couple more."

"And you'd like to have the pageant next Thursday?"

"Yeah. That give you enough time? We want to hold it outside at the garage. We've got a big open lot we can use and decorate. We'll hire a band, and we're good to go."

Six days was plenty of time, and this was the least I could do for Rusty's help on this case. "Okay," I said. "I'd be happy to do that." I handed her one of my cards. "Do you know where the Eberlin House is? That's where I live. Give me a call and we'll set up a time for you all to stop by."

"Deal," she said, and we shook hands again.

Wallie agreed to call me if she thought of anything useful. The women hopped back on their motorcycles and careened off in a cloud of dust. Rusty watched them go and then turned back to me. His brow was furrowed and his tone serious as he addressed his next remarks to Jerry.

"Susie's not the only one who's heard some rumblings around the block. It's not good. You need to watch your back."

"It's that serious?" Jerry said. "Who else is involved?"

Rusty raised his eyebrows at me and cleared his throat in a warning manner.

"It's okay," Jerry said. "She knows all about it."

I had no idea what was going on, but the best course of action was to nod and not say anything.

Even though we were the only people out in the middle of nowhere, Rusty lowered his voice. "The same bunch that's been making noise since the beginning."

"Are they actually planning to make a move?"

"That's what Susie says. You know she's in tight with them. They take out Big Mike, then you're next."

"I never agreed to be next in line," Jerry said.

"They don't know that."

For a long tense moment neither man said anything. I was about to explode with questions.

Then Jerry said, "Thank you."

"No problem," Rusty said. He touched the brim of his hat. "Miss Parkland." He folded himself back into the Corvette and roared away.

There was another long tense moment.

"Okay," I said. "You know how I've often asked you to explain in detail this bizarre code your people have? Today is the day."

"This is all part of Susie's long con," Jerry said. "We've known for a while that a group of Big Mike's former students wanted to take over the organization. Susie pretended to be a part of the revolution and joined this group, specifically to hear what they were planning and pass this information along to Big Mike. According to what Rusty said, they are ready to storm the castle."

"You trust Rusty? You just met him."

"He knew Susie's password," Jerry said as if this solved everything.

Something more disturbing was bothering me. "And what's all this about you being next in line? You never told me that."

"Because I'm no longer next in line. I'm out of the game."

"Yes, but it sounds to me as if this splinter group thinks you're still in."

"Susie will alert me if things start to get serious."

It seemed to me things were serious now. "You never told me you were heir to the throne of Con World."

"Mac." He put his arms around me. "That's because I never wanted the throne. I told Big Mike that a long time ago."

"And he's okay with that?" Big Mike usually got what he wanted, no matter what or who stood in the way.

"He respects my decision, and trust me, he'll take care of the Rebel Alliance. This isn't the first time he's been challenged."

I had to sigh. "I just wanted some useful information about the museum break-in. I didn't expect to get involved in a gang war."

"There won't be a war," Jerry said. "There will be a short decisive battle, Big Mike will win, as always, and you'll have nothing to worry about."

I started to tell him I had plenty to worry about when my phone rang. It was Jake, his voice as bright and cheerful as ever.

"Mystery fire solved! A magician pal of mine said it might be flash paper. I looked into it and he was right. Nothing supernatural, just some kids who bought the rainbow pack. But I've put a major alien spin on it called 'Flash of Death,' so Basil's happy. Got anything for me?"

Let's see. Giant con man in the middle of a trailer park, an all women motorcycle gang, a hostile takeover plot that involved Jerry, and no clues to the missing paintings. I could just imagine the "alien spin" Jake could put on all that.

"Sorry, Jake," I said. "Nothing to report."

***

We'd left Hayden on the porch with his notebook, and I was happy to see he was still there. "Did you find out anything?" he asked.

Jerry was about to pop with his news. "Susie's contact turned out to be one of Mac's fans. Who knew being Miss Parkland could be so useful?"

"That's good, then, isn't it?" Hayden said.

"It's better than having that guy mad at us. He's about the size of this house." He paused, and I heard the faint sound of singing from inside. "Are you still listening to Wagner?"

"Well, I wanted some music, and that CD was in the player,"

Hayden said.

"Come in and check out the next track."

We went into the front parlor, which was now Jerry's music room.

"Here's where Fafner the dragon comes in," Jerry said. "Actually, he's a giant who's taken the form of a dragon."

Hearing the deep echoing tones of the horns, it was possible to believe a dragon was speaking.

Hayden looked at the cover of the CD. "This is the opera that started the cliché of giant women in horned helmets, isn't it?"

"Yep. Brunnhilda. She's the one who's sleeping on a fiery mountain."

"That's actually her name?"

"The other Valkyries have even better names like Helmwiga, Waltrauta, Siegruna, Ortlinda, Schwertleita—gosh, Mac, what great names. Ortlinda Fairweather would be amazing."

"Nope."

"You're making those up," Hayden said.

"Sadly, no. There are a couple more, but I'd have to look them up. Let me find 'Ride of the Valkyries.' That's the best. You may recognize it from a certain Bugs Bunny cartoon."

The hefty strains of the tune I knew as "Kill the Wabbit" blared forth as I hunted in the fridge for a snack. When the music crashed to its finale, Hayden chose something quieter from Jerry's collection, and Jerry came into the kitchen.

"I see you've already started on lunch."

I reached for the pitcher of tea. "All that opera made me hungry."

"Have a seat. I'll whip up a little salad."

I fixed a glass of tea and sat down. "Maybe I'm going about my investigation the wrong way. I don't think an artist would steal their own work. But would they steal each others'? Because they thought they were 'the real artist'?"

"I suppose it's down to whoever has something to benefit."

I thought this over as Jerry chopped up the ingredients for my salad. He handed me the bowl. "French or Thousand Island?"

"French, please, and some cheese."

Jerry fixed salads for himself and Hayden, and we ate on the porch. Austin and Denisha rode up on four-wheeler and bike. They weren't interested in salad, but they were interested in our houseguest.

"Hayden, I believe you know Denisha and Austin," I said.

"Yes, they're in the bookstore all the time," Hayden said.

"We haven't seen you in there lately," Denisha said.

"I'm taking a little break."

"I'm sorry about your mother and your pet. That must be hard."

"It is, thank you, but I have a lot of friends to help me."

"Are you writing something?"

"Pull up a chair. I'll show you."

Austin had other plans. "Hey, Jerry, I bet I can burp louder than you."

"You're on."

"Take it somewhere else," I said.

Jerry and Austin decided to get a couple of colas and burp in the backyard. Denisha was intrigued by Hayden's notebook.

"You wrote all these poems? How many have you written?"

"I lost count a long time ago," he said.

"I'm writing a mystery. *The Mystery of the Missing Charm Bracelet.* Maybe you could read it when I'm done."

"I'd be glad to."

"We wrote poems in my class last year. Want to hear one? "The butterfly has yellow wings, the little robin likes to sing. The trees are budding pink and white. It looks like spring is just in sight.""

"That's beautiful," Hayden said. "I hope you have a copy. It's very important to have more than one copy of your work. Trust me on this."

"Is that what you're doing? Wouldn't it be faster on the computer?"

"Yes, but I can connect better to my words if I write them in ink."

Denisha was fascinated, and Hayden sounded more reasonable than he had in a long time. *This is a good team*, I thought. *They can really help each other.*

Hayden handed Denisha a notebook from the stack by his chair. "Here. You can start your own song cycle. Your spring poem is perfect to begin with. I'll show you."

I checked on the backyard boys. They had apparently burped themselves out and lay sprawled in the grass, arguing over the prowess of certain sports stars. From front porch sublime to backyard ridiculous.

***

That night when Jerry hopped into bed with me, I gave him an ultimatum. "I want to speak to Susie."

He hesitated. "Because?"

"Because it would make me feel better. How about that?"

"Okay," he said. "It might take a day or two to reach her."

"Nope," I said. "Tomorrow."

He didn't answer right away. I raised both eyebrows and gave him my best long stare. He finally nodded. "Will this make up for not telling you about being up for Big Mike's job?"

"Maybe." I pulled him into my arms. "What was that secret password? Over Easy to win?"

"Over Easy it is," he said, and over I went.

CHAPTER NINE

Saturday morning, I spent an hour going over the résumés of the museum board members. I discovered that Letticia and Roxanna had graduated from the same art school, the Mayfield Academy of Art and Design, a very prestigious and expensive school. One I couldn't afford.

I looked up the school and the year the women had attended. Letticia had been the recipient of the Mayfield Scholarship, all expenses paid. She'd been one of the very few to have a showing of her own in the school's private gallery. The "Where Are They Now?" feature in the alumni section listed her as director of the Parkland Museum of Art as well as contributing editor to *Artistic Review*.

Under Roxanna's name there was a short list of her accomplishments, including "Second Place in the Pen and Ink Competition." Her paper on *tromp l'oeil* had been published in *Historical Art Review*, and her diorama on the wetlands of Florida had received an Honorable Mention from the Florida Museum Commission.

Something didn't ring true until I remembered that my mother had said how wealthy Letticia's family was, wealthy enough to send Letticia to any school she chose. Would she even need an all-expenses paid ride?

I gave Mom a call to ask her. "Didn't you tell me Letticia's family was one of the richest families in Parkland?"

"Yes, that's right."

"Letticia got a full scholarship to Mayfield Academy."

"I don't see what's wrong with that. I'm sure she deserved it. Are you any closer to finding the paintings, Madeline? Do you have any suspects, at all?"

"I'm coming to Parkland to talk with Letticia again," I said. "I'll stop by and visit you."

"That won't be necessary," she said. "Armand is coming to fix my hair this morning. This is the only time he can come, and he's charging me extra."

"Is something wrong at his salon?"

"No, but I'm just not ready to face the women who will be there."

It was hard to keep the amusement out of my voice. "So Armand is paying a house call?" I could not imagine the fussy Frenchman leaving his salon to his minions.

My mother's reply was as stiff as Armand would style her hair. "I am doing what I can to remain calm, Madeline."

"All right," I said. "I'll see you later."

***

I found Letticia in the main gallery of the museum. She and Roxanna were standing in front of a large display that took up the entire hallway. It resembled a museum of the past.

"You need to relax," Roxanna was saying. "I know a lot of things have been upsetting lately, but this is going to be finished on time, I promise."

"I wish I could have your confidence," Letticia replied. "Since the playground equipment won't be here for the Children's Festival, it's vitally important this exhibit is ready. Oh, hello, Madeline."

"Good morning," I said. "This looks interesting."

"This is how the Parkland Museum of Art looked in the Thirties," she said. "We're doing a retrospective for National Museum Month."

The exhibit looked as if you could step inside another time. There were ornate chairs, little tables with Chinese vases, and paintings on the walls in matching thick wooden frames.

"Roxanna does beautiful work," Letticia said.

"It's really lovely," I said. "It looks finished to me."

"No, but it will be," Roxanna said. "I told Letticia she doesn't have a thing to worry about."

"Except the late grant, the playground, the fake Halsey painting, and especially the missing paintings," Letticia said. "Any news, Madeline?"

"Maybe. Who has access to your office?"

"Anyone can come in."

"And this might sound odd, but did the police search the museum? Closets, storage areas, the Dumpsters out back?"

"Yes, actually they did search the storage areas and all around outside."

One of the docents approached. "Letticia, Doug Elmore would like to speak with you in your office."

Letticia didn't look too pleased by this news. "Excuse me, Madeline," she said and followed the docent out.

Roxanna rearranged one of the vases. "She's going to have a nervous breakdown if she doesn't look out."

"Do you think so?"

"I've known her a long time. She's high-strung. I told her I'd be glad to take over some of the museum duties, but she feels like she has to do it all or it's not done right. Of course, I feel that way about my displays, so I really can't say anything. Nobody's touching them but me. 'A Walk Back in Time.' That's what I'm going to call this."

"It's very impressive." I gave the display another look. As with most art museums in the Thirties, paintings were influenced by the Great Depression and Franklin Roosevelt's Public Works of Art Project, the first federal program to support the arts. Artists were encouraged to create works depicting the "American Scene" to lift everyone's spirits. The Parkland Art Museum had a typical collection of cityscapes, landscapes, and rural scenes, all filled with movement, strong lines, and rounded forms: people gathering at a railroad station, boats with billowing sails, workers at a printing press.

"These are wonderful," I said. Something about the paintings jogged a memory, but I couldn't place it.

"These are only few of our best ones," Roxanna said. "I didn't have room for them all."

Maybe it would come to me later. "You say you've known Letticia a long time. I understand you and she were classmates at Mayfield Academy."

I didn't miss the annoyed expression that flitted across her face. "Yes, that's where we met. I'm not sure why she chose Mayfield when she could afford to go anywhere."

"Wasn't there a scholarship involved?"

Now Roxanna was more than annoyed. "A scholarship she didn't deserve and certainly didn't need. But I managed to do quite well on my own, even if it meant working extra shifts at the local diner."

Did that explain her contempt for the waiters at the museum coffee shop? "So no hard feelings?"

"That was a long time ago." She gestured to the display. "I'm getting to do what I want, and I'm very good at it." Her phone rang and she checked the number. "Oh, of all the stupid women I have to deal with, this one's the worst. Excuse me, Madeline."

I was happy to leave her as she berated some hapless assistant for her lack of proper wallpaper for the display.

I'd hoped to have a few more words with Letticia, but as I approached her office, I heard voices that alerted me she and Doug Elmore were still meeting. Letticia sounded exasperated.

"Doug, I assure you, everything's taken care of."

His voice was also exasperated and much more strident. "That's what you said about the grant and the forged Halsey and especially the break-in. I told you we should have gone with Safety First."

"And I believe I told you they wanted too much money."

"They're the best security company in town."

"As you'll recall our finance director said we couldn't afford them."

"And look what happened." He didn't wait for her to reply. "I've been talking with some of the other board members, and we think it's time you handed over the running of this museum to someone more competent."

Now her voice was icy calm. "That would be up to the board

to decide."

"Which is why I'm here. I wanted to let you know ahead of time we plan to call a special meeting to discuss this matter."

"Fine," she said.

"It's nothing personal. You know we want only the best for the museum."

"Of course. Do you and the others have someone in mind for the director's position?"

"We haven't discussed that."

There was a long moment of silence. Then Doug Elmore said, "I'll let you know when the meeting's scheduled."

On his way out of the office, he saw me and gave a brief nod. "Ms. Maclin. Any news on the robbery?"

"Nothing so far," I said.

"That's unfortunate, but I'm sure you're doing all you can."

With that, he walked off. I waited a moment and then knocked on the open office door. "I couldn't help but hear," I said. "Are you all right?"

She was standing beside her desk, both fists clenched. "He only wants the best for the museum, he says. He means himself."

"He wants your job?"

"He won't get it. He doesn't have the qualifications. But he's been opposed to me since I began."

"Any particular reason why?"

"Oh, I don't know." She shook out her hands. "My god, he gets on my nerves." She sat down behind her desk. "He's one of those people who thinks he knows everything. I'm sorry, Madeline, did you want to speak with me?"

I took the seat opposite. "Does he have enough support on the board to have you replaced?"

"No. But he can make things so unpleasant I may have to re-sign."

"Don't do that," I said. "Let me keep looking. Doug Elmore has a key to the museum. I'd like to know where he was Tuesday night."

She paused. "The break-in? You think he could have some-thing to do with that? But that's crazy. Isn't it?"

"I've seen crazier things," I said. "And while we're talking about hostile board member takeovers, what's your relationship like with Roxanna?"

"A bit stormy. We met at college. She always felt her work was better than anyone else's and didn't take criticism well, at all. She was up for the director's job, too, and not happy when I got it. But she's thrilled to be able to create whatever she likes for the museum."

I'm getting to do what I want and I'm very good at it. That's what Roxanna had told me. So maybe she was thrilled. Maybe she wasn't plotting to get Letticia's job. Maybe I needed a closer look at Doug Elmore.

***

I got into my car and checked my watch. Doug might not have had enough time to get back to Parson's Creek, but it wouldn't hurt to talk to Dawn. In fact, it might be better. She seemed more sympathetic to Letticia's situation.

Dawn was sitting on their front porch, Dixie lounging beside her rocking chair. As soon as I got out of my car, the little dog leaped up and ran in furious circles around the yard. Dawn tried to catch her, but she insisted on hurling herself at me like a mini-tornado. When Dawn bent down to catch her she transferred her energy to snapping at Dawn's ankles.

"Dixie!" Dawn grabbed the wiggling dog, who rolled over on her back, tongue dangling, the very picture of a cute puppy. "Oh, that won't work with me." She scooped Dixie up. "I don't suppose you'd like to have a dog, Ms Maclin?"

"It's Madeline, please," I said. Dixie let me pat her head. "She's just excited."

"She's driving us crazy," Dawn said. "She belonged to my mother, and when Mother went into a nursing home, we were stuck with the dog. I thought she'd settle down, but, as you can see, she's wild. Let me put her in the house."

Once Dixie was corralled, we sat down in the rocking chairs.

Dawn fanned herself with the magazine she'd been reading.

"Now, what can I do for you? I hope you have good news about the paintings."

"I wish I did," I said. "What can you tell me about Safety First?"

There was a whack as Dixie hit the door from inside.

"Stop that," Dawn told the dog. "Oh, that's the company Doug used to work for. He was not happy when they didn't get the contract for the museum."

Well, that explained that. "So Doug knows about security systems?"

"Yes, he worked in the security business for twenty-five years. He knows everything there is to know about alarms and video surveillance and things like that. He told Letticia the keys they were using were not the best."

"Why didn't the museum go with Safety First?" I asked.

"Some sort of budget concern. I think Letticia spent too much on the porcelains she purchased last month and on the statuary for the outdoor garden. But the board voted on all these things and the majority won." Another whack and a whine. "Dixie, quit it."

"Do you think someone else should be the museum director?"

She took a while to answer. "I like Letticia. I think she's doing a good job. But after a while, you have to take into consideration what's best for the museum, and maybe it's time to get someone new."

"Someone like Doug?"

"He and I have talked about it, but I'm not sure it's the right job for him. That's up to the board, of course."

A third whack made the door shudder. Dixie let us know what she thought about being inside with a series of sharp barks.

"She's ready to explode," Dawn said. "Sure you don't want a dog?"

A dog, maybe, but not a Tasmanian Devil. "No, thanks."

***

Since my mother had given me strict instructions to stay away until Armand had worked his magic, I decided to go home. I found Jerry sitting on the porch steps talking with a small blond woman with tiny features and big blue eyes. I knew right away this was Sobbin' Susie. Both of them stood to greet me.

"I was just getting ready to call you, Mac," Jerry said. "I'd like you to meet Sobbin' Susie. Susie, this is my wife, Madeline Maclin."

Susie barely came up to my shoulder. With her blond bowl cut and bangs and plain blue dress, she looked like a ten-year-old child from the 1950s. Even her little voice was childlike. "Pleasure to meet you, Madeline."

"Susie's agreed to explain a few things," Jerry said.

"All right," I said. "Why don't we move to the kitchen? I'm going to need some coffee."

We sat down at the kitchen table, and everyone had a cup of coffee.

Susie set her coffee cup down. "You realize, Madeline, I can't tell you everything. But Big Mike's organization is facing some serious threats, and I'm playing a long con. That's a con that can go on for months, even years. Jerry doesn't know the details because he's not involved. Hopefully, if this con works, he won't have to be."

"But you've been calling him with messages about everything rolling along," I said.

She smiled, all traces of ten-year-old gone. "That's for anyone else who might be listening in. Jerry's my cover."

I wasn't sure I liked this. "So, you're pretending to run one con with Jerry, but you're actually doing another unrelated con?"

"Yes, exactly, in hopes of finding out who's trying to take over Big Mike's organization."

I took another drink, wishing I had something stronger than coffee. "But who'd dare challenge Big Mike?"

"That's a very good question. You'd think his people would stay loyal to him, but unfortunately, people get greedy."

And stupid, I thought.

"No leads?" Jerry asked.

"It's better if you don't know. Actually, coming to visit you works in my favor. If anyone's watching me, they'll figure this is all about our con."

"Which is?" I asked.

"Can't tell you that, either, but it's harmless." She grinned.

"You got any other questions I can't answer?"

So many questions. "What if Jerry has to get involved? These people you're conning, they think he's the next Big Mike, don't they? What's to keep them from coming after him?"

"Well, me, for one thing," she said. "Plus all the people I've got on my side, like Rusty. And the minute Big Mike finds out who's trying to take over, he'll come down on them like a hammer. A really big hammer. You've got nothing to worry about."

I wished everyone would quit saying that. "I appreciate you stopping by."

"Oh, I'd do anything for Jerry."

"Show her what you're famous for," he said.

"Sure."

She blinked her eyes a few times and they rapidly filled with tears, tears that ran down her cheeks and spilled onto the table, continuing to gush until she wiped her eyes with a napkin. Like a magic trick, the tears went away.

"Comes in real handy in a variety of situations," she said. "Lost child, devastated widow, upset wife, angry girlfriend. Name it and I can sob on cue."

"That's impressive," I said.

"When you're small like me, you have to improvise. Jerry, I'd better get going. Nice to meet you, Mac. I won't see you again."

"I understand."

She got into her beige Taurus and drove off. I turned Jerry's face to mine so I could kiss him. "Thanks for breaking the Sacred Code for me."

He tugged at one of my many uncooperative curls. "Might have bent it a little. What do you want to do now? Have you heard from Jake this morning?"

Right on cue, my phone rang. But it wasn't Jake. It was Joanie Raines. I hadn't heard from her since she stopped by my office to complain about Amanda Price and the on-going outdoor drama feud.

"Madeline, you have to do something! The money for our show is missing, and so is Amanda! We think she ran off with our funds! You have to come to the Rossboro Arts Council building right away. It's on the park across from the city hall building."

"Joanie, that's not really my—"

"You have to come!" she said. "I told them you could solve this."

"Okay, calm down," I said. "I'll see what I can do." She thanked me and I ended the call. "Looks like the rest of my morning has been decided," I told Jerry. "We're on our way to Rossboro."

"Now what?" he said, amused.

"More outdoor drama."

CHAPTER TEN

Jerry and I had been to Rossboro before to meet with a lawyer who had information for me that helped unravel a riddle for another client. Unfortunately, this same lawyer had been a victim of one of Jerry's past schemes, and she sent her giant boyfriend to the Eberlin House to have a word with him. After that, we decided to limit our visits to Rossboro.

The park Joanie mentioned was the main feature of the town, a truly beautiful square with walkways and bike trails and a court-yard under ancient oak trees. A large fountain sat in the center, water splashing from the mouths of smiling stone dolphins. The park also had a soccer field, a baseball diamond, and tennis courts. Surrounding the park were several buildings. A few were restored historic buildings and others were new. The new buildings includ-ed an amphitheater, city hall, and the Arts Council. Joanie stood out front, and when she saw us, she waved.

Jerry found a parking spot in the Arts Council lot, and we bare-ly had time to get out of the car before Joanie rushed up.

"Thank you for coming! I didn't want to get the police involved until we were absolutely sure Amanda took the money."

"What makes you think she did?" I asked.

"Because she had a huge argument with the director last night and said the show was going to go her way or not at all. Then just a little while ago when the woman who's handling the funds did some checking, she said nearly five thousand dollars is gone. Who else would take it? Come inside and talk to everyone."

The Rossboro Theater was much larger than Celosia's Baker Auditorium with recessed lighting and golden walls. I estimated the room would seat several hundred people. The light and sound boards looked like something you'd find on the bridge of the *Enterprise*. The stage was immense. On this stage stood three people, a man and two women, and all three looked highly annoyed. All three had basically the same story. The director said Amanda was impossible to work with. The stage manager said she argued with him about everything. The woman in charge of money said she'd never met anyone so disagreeable and why hadn't Amanda stayed in Celosia?

When Amanda was my client, she was impossible, argumentative, and disagreeable, so I sympathized. What these people didn't know about Amanda was that even though she'd had money, she was now broke, which was one of the reasons she'd put her huge house up for sale and left Celosia. Was she desperate enough to take the Arts Council money?

"When was the last time you saw Amanda?" I asked.

"Last night at rehearsal," the director said. "She insisted on having our playwright write another scene for her. The show is already too long, and believe me, I would love to cut her completely out, so there's no way she's getting another scene. Besides, it doesn't make sense to have the village seamstress on stage forever."

"That's her part? Village seamstress?" Quite a come down from playing Emmaline in Celosia's production.

"She thought by moving here, she could be the star, but that's not how things work in Rossboro."

"Where does she live? Has anyone been by her house?"

"She's staying in the Crescent View Townhouses," Joanie said. "I've been over there twice, and there's no sign of her or her car."

"You should go to the police."

"No, no, it would be bad publicity for the show. Right now, only the people standing here on the stage know about this. We need to take care of the problem before the newspaper gets wind of it. Please, Madeline."

I agreed to take the case. "Tell me how to get to the Crescent View Townhouses. Maybe Jerry and I can find some clues at

Amanda's apartment."

Joanie walked us out. "Thank you so much. I know you didn't have to help me since I set Rossboro against Celosia."

Way too dramatic. "The towns aren't at war, Joanie. I'm sure the two shows will be completely different."

Joanie didn't want to let go. "Still, there's bound to be bad blood. You see how Amanda planned this, don't you?"

Amanda was manipulative, but I didn't think she was a thief. "We'll figure it out."

***

The Crescent View Townhouses were rows and rows of neat brick homes each with its own front porch and upstairs balcony. Jerry eyed the balcony of Amanda's house.

"That won't be a problem."

"Let's see if we can get in legally first."

We checked under the welcome mat, in the mailbox, and under several likely-looking rocks for a key. We went around to the back door and met the next door neighbor coming out to refill her birdfeeder. I greeted her and said I was a friend of Amanda's and disappointed she wasn't home.

The neighbor poured a cup of seeds into the feeder. "Oh, she's moved."

"Oh, no, really? When was this?"

"Oh, there was quite a racket around three AM this morning. I saw a U-Haul truck parked out front and a couple of men putting furniture in it, so I assume she moved out. Why she couldn't wait until a decent hour, I don't know. Can't say I'm sorry she's gone. Don't want to say anything bad about her, but if you're really a friend of hers, then you know how she is."

"Yes, she can be difficult."

"Rude's what I'd call it. Didn't like me having a feeder out here because she said the birds made too much noise. Little birds cheeping, and she's upset."

Jerry tried the back door. "Is there a spare key anywhere? One of the reasons we're here is to pick up my wife's punchbowl.

Amanda borrowed it a few months ago for a party."

"She probably took it with her. Check by the office, number four twenty six. They'll let you in."

"Nice story," I said to Jerry as we walked down to the townhouse office.

"If I'd known we were going to do some breaking and entering, I would've brought my special keys."

"I thought you always had them on you."

"Trying to reform, Mac, trying to reform."

The townhouse manager confirmed that Amanda had moved out, and he'd be glad to let us in to look for the phantom punchbowl.

"Was this move sudden?" I asked.

"Yes, and she broke her lease."

"Any idea where she was going?"

He was as disgusted as the next door neighbor about Amanda's behavior. "No, she stole away in the night."

Amanda's townhouse was bare and chilly. The only things she'd left behind were the living room curtains, a roll of paper towels, and a plastic trash can filled with papers, rags, and a broken picture frame.

"Do you mind if we look through the trash?" I asked the manager. "There might be a clue as to where she went."

"Go right ahead. I'd love to know where she is."

While Jerry and I rooted through the trash can, the manager walked through the townhouse, no doubt assessing what he'd need to do to get the place in shape for the next tenant. The only thing we found that could possibly be a clue was a scrap of paper with "10 AM FBC, Parkland" written on it and another scribbled note that said, "Ask about third tier."

"Third tier?" Jerry said. "Did she want a seat in the Parkland Coliseum for the hockey game?"

"Does the Rossboro amphitheater have tiers?"

"I don't think it's that big."

But something else had tiers. "Wedding cakes." I stared. "FBC Parkland. First Baptist Church. Jerry, I'll bet you anything she's getting married again."

"We'd better find the poor guy and warn him."

We thanked the manager and promised to let him know when we found Amanda. Then we jumped in the car and hurried to the First Baptist Church in Parkland. Of course, we had no way of knowing which day at 10 AM Amanda's note meant, but the pastor would know.

Jerry frowned at the scrap of paper. "How could she put together a wedding so fast? Don't women spend years planning the perfect day?"

"This is Amanda Price we're talking about. If she wants something, she gets it."

"FBC might mean something else."

"I spent enough time in Parkland to recognize those initials. First Baptist is the biggest church in town."

First Baptist Church was a huge pile of gray stone and stained glass windows with a massive steeple jutting up from the roof like a NASA rocket preparing for takeoff. Once we found the right door that led to the office, we caught a lucky break. A pleasant woman pastor told us she'd met with Amanda at ten one morning last week. As far as she knew Amanda hadn't planned on a ceremony in the church, but had rented one of the many fellowship halls for a reception at three on Sunday.

"Would you happen to know the groom?" I asked.

"Oh, yes, he's a member here. Anderson Stratton. A very nice man. I'm so glad he's found someone."

Mr. Stratton might revise his opinion once he'd lived with Amanda for a while.

We thanked the pastor and left.

Jerry looked hopeful. "Are we going to crash the reception? We could use the punchbowl excuse again."

"We might have to."

"I'm all out of ideas right now. Let's eat something."

***

Since we were in Parkland, there was no question where we'd go. Baxter's Barbecue, home of the best barbecue in the world and our favorite hangout. The best thing about Baxter's was it never changed. It always had the same wooden booths, the same rickety chairs, the same tables covered with plastic red and white checked tablecloths, the same white plastic forks and metal napkin dispensers, even the same waitresses bustling about calling everybody "Honey." Of course, the main attraction was the juicy pork barbecue crammed into white bread buns with tangy slaw and crunchy hushpuppies, all washed down with very sweet iced tea.

Jerry and I had worked our way through a sandwich and a half each before we paused for air.

I reached for another napkin. "Well, I've got a couple of possibilities for who's behind the museum break-in. Roxanna might be happy creating displays, or she might still be harboring a serious jealousy grudge, and Doug Elmore, who would like to run the museum himself and knows all about security systems."

"Can we assume Roxanna would also know how the surveillance system works?"

"I imagine Roxanna knows all about the museum. But so do a lot of people." I used a hushpuppy to wipe up a dollop of barbecue sauce that had escaped the bun. "I wish I could get a grip on this case. I think if the Valkyries came flying out of the sky right now, I would definitely thumb a ride back to Valhalla."

"You'd have to sing the battle song."

"Don't think I won't. I need a battle song."

"It's mainly 'Hoyotoho' and 'Heiaha.'"

"There's more, isn't there?"

Of course there was more. Thankfully, Jerry kept it low. "'Fly then swiftly and speed to the east! Bravely determine all trials to bear. Hunger and thirst, thorns and hard ways, Smile through all pain while suffering pangs!'"

"Ow. Tough gals."

"Yep, like you. You can handle it."

"I know. I just wish I had more to go on." As if waiting for this cue, my cell phone rang. "Now that's probably Jake." But once again it wasn't Jake. I didn't recognize the number. However, I recognized the deep friendly tones of Big Mike.

"Madeline, my dear. I hope this finds you well."

Oh, my God, I mouthed at Jerry. "Yes, thank you, Big Mike."

Jerry dropped his sandwich, his eyes wide.

"Jerry and I are fine, thanks. We're working on a case."

"I heard about your missing painting. I'm very sorry and hope you find it soon, but that's not the reason I called. There's a little matter we need to settle."

Of course, on top of everything else, Big Mike decided now was the time to call in the favor. I hoped my voice sounded calm. "What can I do for you?"

"I attended a dinner party the other night, a fund raiser for the Parkland Library, and I overheard a discussion regarding a Cecille Maclin. Further discreet questions revealed that she is your mother."

After I processed Big Mike and Parkland Library, I thought, *Where in the world is this conversation going?* "That's right."

"Apparently, some people are concerned about her connection to the museum break-in."

"Yes, she's very upset about the effect this is having on her social standing."

"I'd like for you to introduce me to your mother."

My brain took several moments to reboot. I must have looked stunned because Jerry said, "Mac? Are you okay?"

"I'd be delighted," I told Big Mike, "but I have to warn you, she's nothing like me."

"Jerry was amazingly lucky to snag you first."

"Thank you. But my mother hasn't wanted any sort of male company for as long as I can remember."

"Quite all right. I enjoy a challenge."

By now, Jerry had figured out what was going on, and I'm sure his stunned expression mirrored mine.

Big Mike had it all planned. "You know the Elms, I'm sure. I'll be there tomorrow at noon. I'm looking forward to meeting your mother and to seeing you again. Tell Jerry to come along, too. We'll make it a double date."

What else could I do but agree? "Okay, then, tomorrow at noon." He ended the call. I stared at my phone.

Jerry tapped my hand to get my attention. "Did Big Mike just ask you to hook him up with your mother?"

"Yes, he did. We have a double date with them tomorrow at the Elms."

He sat back. "I have now officially heard everything."

When Big Mike told me I owed him for getting Jerry out of the Derek situation, I never considered he'd want anything so innocuous. But convincing my mother to come to lunch with a man—any man—was going to be as tough as any underworld deal I could imagine. "Why do you suppose he wants me to do that?"

"He likes the ladies, and Cecille's not a bad-looking woman."

"Yes, but, Jerry, she never goes out. Her relationship with my father must have been volcanic, because she doesn't want to have anything to do with men."

"Big Mike's a charmer. He might be the one." He started to laugh. "He's going to make one hell of a stepfather."

"Stop. This is crazy. He must have an ulterior motive."

"Of course he does. He always does. But as favors go, you got off light."

My delicious Baxter's barbecue meal was no longer appealing. "What could he possibly want?"

"Maybe he wants to help solve the break-in at the museum. If he helps to clear Cecille's name, she might warm up to him."

"Until she finds out what he does for a living."

"Oh, he can put a spin on that like you wouldn't believe."

"All this doesn't matter because I very seriously doubt she'll want to meet him."

"Call her and find out."

The first thing Mom wanted to know was if I had found the missing paintings. "Why don't we meet for lunch tomorrow and have a nice long discussion about everything?" I said.

"Where do you want to go?"

"How about the Elms? It's quiet, and I'll reserve a table in a private area. You need to get out of the house, Mom."

"I suppose."

"Jerry will be there and a friend of his, if that's all right."

"If Jerry and his friend are there, I don't see how we can discuss sensitive matters."

"Jerry's friend might be able to help find the paintings."

She made an annoyed huffing sound. "You know, Madeline, I've been hearing things about Jerry's friends that do not make me comfortable with this idea."

"Would you please come and hear what he has to say? He's really very nice."

"What's his name?"

This caught me off-guard. I only knew him as Big Mike. "His name?" I signaled frantically to Jerry. What do I say?

"Tell her Michael Crown," he said.

"His name is Michael Crown, Mom, and he's a businessman."

"Why does he need to be there? You can get your information from him at another time, can't you?"

"He's only going to stop by for a few minutes." Jerry raised his eyebrows at this, but I had to say something. "Please, Mom. It'll really help my investigation." I held my breath until I heard her sigh.

"Very well."

"Jerry and I will pick you up at eleven thirty." I gave her my love and hung up. I sat back in my chair. "Two phone calls and I feel completely done in for the day."

"But she said yes."

"You heard me. I had to lie. I'm sure Big Mike's real name isn't Michael Crown. Is Crown for King of the Con Men?"

"It's short for crown and anchor, an illegal and highly profitable dice game."

"So not Michael Roulette, or Michael Royal Flush?"

"Or Michael Craps."

We laughed so hard the waitress came over to make sure we were all right. A big burst of laughter did a lot to relieve my tension, and I was able to finish my sandwich as well as an extra helping of hushpuppies.

CHAPTER ELEVEN

Hayden had been asleep all morning, but when we got home, he and Denisha were on the porch. They had exchanged their notebooks for peanut butter sandwiches.

"I hope you don't mind, but we raided your kitchen," Hayden said.

"No problem," Jerry said. "Did you find the chips? I'll get them."

Denisha held up her notebook. "Madeline, I've written five poems."

"That's fantastic."

"And I've written two," Hayden said. "I believe Denisha is my new muse."

"Muse?" she said. "What's that?"

"Someone who is an inspiration." At her little frown, he clarified. "Someone who helps me come up with ideas."

"Oh, well, I'm good at that. I help Austin come up with ideas all the time."

"Any leads on your painting, Madeline?" he asked.

"Nothing yet. I haven't had any more calls, have I?"

"No, nothing. I'm sorry."

Jerry came back with the chips in time to hear Denisha explain Austin's absence.

"He's at the dirt track all day. He is so crazy about that new four-wheeler. But we're going out to the haunted house later."

Hayden stopped eating. "What haunted house?"

"Old Man Tumpty's place. Austin's sure there're zombies in it."

Even Hayden found this hard to believe. "What makes him say that?"

"He just likes to make stuff up. Everybody knows zombies don't live around here."

"They don't live at all," Jerry said. "If the house is in bad shape, you guys shouldn't be playing in it."

"We're just going to look. You're coming, aren't you? You can come, too, Hayden."

"Sounds like fun, but I'm staying right here," he said.

Denisha's aunt called to remind Denisha of a friend's birthday party. Denisha thanked Hayden for the notebook and for his help. She hopped on her bike and rode off across the field.

Hayden smiled as he watched Denisha go. I hoped she wasn't distracting him from his work. "We really enjoy having Denisha around, but she'll understand if you want to be alone."

"No, it was very nice having some company," Hayden said. "We worked on our poems and talked about our mothers. Denisha's passed away when Denisha was three. She said she has a picture of her mother she likes, but she never really knew her, and she said I was lucky to have had mine for so long. We're also both only children and agree that's not a bad thing. She wrote a lovely poem about her mother's picture." He turned a page in his notebook. "I thought I might write a poem about my mother. It would be a different direction for me."

I'd read Hayden's poems. They could be a bit obscure. "Poems about mothers always resonate with people."

"That's true. Maybe my work needs to be more emotionally accessible."

Jerry's cell phone rang. He answered, listened, and then said, "Sure, now's good. Thanks." He ended the call. "Your Pageantoid is on the way with the Angels."

I had a mouthful of tea and almost did a spit take. "What? Now? I thought he and the gang were going to set up a time."

Jerry's eyes were alight with mischief. "Guess the time is now. And Rusty's got a program he wants you to sign."

"A Pageantoid?" Hayden said.

"That's what I call Mac's more rabid fans," Jerry said. "Rusty's the one I told you about. Wait till you see this guy. He's got arms bigger than both of us put together. He'd make a terrific zombie hunter. Watch for a red Corvette."

In about ten minutes, the Corvette roared up the driveway and spun neatly to park under a tree. Hayden was impressed by the spectacle of Rusty embarking from the sports car.

"You weren't kidding," he said to Jerry.

"Check out the tattoos."

Rusty's red Corvette was followed by Helen's Angels on their motorcycles. The women parked their bikes under one of the trees in the front yard and strolled up to the porch. "The tall woman with the black braid is Helga," I told Hayden. "She appears to be the leader. The little woman is Wallie, the dark woman with copper hair is Orla and the blond twins are Sissy and Leeta."

"They are amazingly attractive and frightening at the same time," he said.

Rusty came up the porch steps. He didn't take off his sunglasses or his hat. Jerry introduced him to Hayden, and Rusty introduced the women.

Orla gave Hayden a narrow-eyed look. "You're Hayden Amry?"

"Yes," he said apprehensively.

"Author of *Glass Plums*?"

Definitely not what he expected. "You've read *Glass Plums*?"

She beamed at him. "Thought I recognized you from your picture on the back of the book. Yeah, I've read it, and so has Leeta."

Leeta chomped on her gum. "Yeah, it was cool."

Hayden managed to say, "Thank you."

Rusty turned his blank gaze to me. "Madeline, the ladies thought you could give them a few pointers this afternoon."

Jerry offered to bring out more chairs, but the women waved him off and took seats on the porch steps.

Helga tossed her black braid over her shoulder. "We just stopped by to get the basics. What sort of stuff to wear, how to walk and stand. We've seen enough pageants on TV to know most of it."

"I'll be glad to show you," I said.

"We already know we'll do swimsuits," Orla said. "Maybe evening gown, if there's time. Maybe talent. Only stupid talent, you know, like chewing gum or standing on one foot."

"I can't even do that," Leeta said, and her sister guffawed and slapped her shoulder.

"Not at the same time, that's for damn sure."

"We've come with some names for ourselves," Helga said. "I'm Miss Gear Shift, Wallie's Miss Overdrive, Orla's Miss Spark Plug, and I don't know what the other two's decided."

"Miss Tail Pipe and Miss Lube Job," one twin said, and they fell over laughing.

"Keep it clean," Rusty said.

"Rusty, you are so boring," the other twin said.

"What do you think, Madeline?" he asked. "Can you do anything with this bunch?"

In my opinion, these women were a lot more fun than any of the ladies I'd had to contend with backstage. "I think this pageant is going to be epic."

We went out to the front yard, and I showed the Miss Streetwise contestants how to walk, how to pose at the end of the runway, how to stand and turn, and how to wave. The practice was a welcome diversion after the upset of the morning. Jerry, Hayden, and Rusty willingly sat on the top porch step as judges, and the women tried a variety of ridiculous talents before settling on their favorites. Jerry fixed cookies and sodas for everyone which they enjoyed on a tablecloth picnic style in the shade of the trees. Then he and Hayden admired the motorcycles. The women were eager to talk about their vehicles. At one point, all I could see were rear ends as they peered down at the gleaming engines.

Sissy and Leeta shrieked with laughter at something Jerry said. Rusty's gaze narrowed as he replaced his sunglasses. "Those two better watch it."

"It's okay," I said.

"You two really trust each other, don't you? That's nice." He indicated Orla with her hand on Hayden's shoulder as they looked into the depths of the engine. "What about that? The girls have taken a shine to him. It's not every day you meet a real live poet.

Didn't think there were any left."

"He's happily married to a very beautiful successful woman. No problems there."

"If you say so."

Wallie left the group and came to me. "Madeline, I thought of something that might help you find our paintings."

"I'll take all the help I can get," I said.

"There's this guy I used to go out with, Zack Turner. He's not a painter. He's a sculptor. We didn't have much of a relationship because he started seeing another girl. Anyway, his mother is head of the Parkland Museum of Art and maybe he knows something."

"What makes you say that?"

She shrugged. "He was always so pissed because his mom wouldn't give him special treatment. I found that kind of behavior really stupid and juvenile, and besides he wasn't that great of a boyfriend. So maybe he took the paintings to get back at her."

"How would he get in?"

"He knew a back door that didn't lock properly. We went in one time after hours. He thought it was a big deal to show me, but I didn't like the idea of being in the museum when nobody was there. 'What if we get caught?' I asked him, and he said, 'It's no big deal. My mother runs the place.'"

"Didn't an alarm go off?"

"No, he went to this panel and put in some numbers and said it was all clear."

Hmm. Zack had told me he didn't know how to get into the museum. Not only could he get in, he knew how to turn off the security system. "Thanks," I said. "I'll look into that."

"He'll talk to you," Wallie said. "He doesn't want to have anything to do with me, and the feeling's mutual."

Rusty made a "humph!" sound. "I'd better not catch that loser anywhere around." He heaved himself up. "We'd better go." I signed Rusty's program. He gave me his phone number. "You be careful, Miss Parkland. Call if you need me. All right, ladies! Head 'em up."

The women thanked me and hopped onto their vehicles. After an excessive revving of engines, they roared back down the driveway, the Corvette close behind.

Hayden gathered up the plastic cups while I folded the table-cloth. "That was not what I expected," he said.

Jerry handed me the cookie plate. "But a fun afternoon, right?"

"Fun and possibly profitable," I said. "Wallie had a few strong words to say about Zack Turner."

He started to pick up the empty cans and paused. "Something just occurred to me. The ladies' names."

"Typical Southern names, except for Helga."

"Something else. I can't figure it."

"You may not call our baby Helga. Or Wallie."

Hayden stacked the plastic cups together. "Helga's a German name, isn't it? She didn't look like a Helga."

Jerry snapped his fingers. "That's it! They're all Valkyrie sisters."

What was he talking about? "I know you had your head under a motorcycle or two. Did you inhale fumes of some kind?"

"Don't you get it? Their names match the Valkyries' crazy names. Helga is Helmwiga, Wallie is Waltrauta, Orla is Ortlinda. Let's see. I know I can make this work. Sissy is Siegruna, and Lee-ta's Schwertleita. All we need now is a Brunnhilda. Whoa, hang on. Didn't you tell me Wallie's painting is called *Fire on the Mountain*?"

"Jerry." I put the tablecloth on a rocking chair. "The operas you listen to often have eerie correlations to my cases, but this is way too far-fetched."

"This is great. This is perfect. They came charging up on their wild rides, fierce warrior women of the street. They wanted to carry you off, didn't they, Hayden? Only you aren't dead yet."

"They were extremely friendly."

"I'll say."

He was having too much fun with this. I checked my watch. "Call it what you like. It was a nice distraction, but it's time to pay Zack Turner another visit."

CHAPTER TWELVE

A silver Honda Accord was parked in front of Zack's studio, but Zack was not in his usual place out front chipping away on a rock. Muffled ooh and ahh sounds led us around to the back of his studio where we found Zack involved in another pursuit with a partially clothed Roxanna Deluca. As soon as the lovers realized we were there, they broke apart. Zack hastily smoothed back his untidy hair, and Roxanna made an attempt to button her blouse.

"Madeline, what a surprise," she said as calmly as if I'd interrupted afternoon tea. "I didn't hear you come in."

"Sorry to interrupt. We can come back later."

She didn't look as witchy with her hair mussed and her makeup askew. "No, no. I was just leaving." She gave Zack a quick kiss. "See you later."

When she'd gone, Zack looked at us as if we'd whipped out our phones and videoed his little escapade. "I'd appreciate it if you wouldn't mention this to Phoebe. I don't think she'd understand."

"That you're playing *The Graduate* with her and her mother? Yes, that would be hard to figure out."

He tucked in his shirt. "She's going to help me with my career, that's all. She likes to sponsor talented artists and authors, creative people of all kinds."

"I think there's more to it than that."

He glared at me. "Why are you here? What do you want?"

Jerry wandered off. "I'm just having a look around," he said.

"I want to know about Wallace Everly," I said.

This surprised him. "What's there to know? We dated for a while."

"Until you started seeing Phoebe."

"Yeah, so what? It didn't work out with Wallie, that's all. You got some sort of strange interest in my love life all of a sudden?"

"One of the stolen paintings belongs to Wallie," I said. "But of course, you knew that, didn't you?"

He eyed me apprehensively. "I knew she painted, sure."

"*Fire on the Mountain* was chosen for the gala exhibit."

"Yeah, so?"

"Were you jealous? Jealous enough to steal her painting?"

Jerry had circled back around, and with a slight shake of his head indicated to me he hadn't found anything.

Zack lost his temper. "I had nothing to do with that! I was angry that the committee only wanted paintings for the gala, yes. I was ticked off that Wallie's painting got in, yes. But Roxanna's going to get me a show of my own. I'm sorry about Wallie's painting and yours, but I had nothing to do with the robbery!"

"Does Phoebe know about you and Roxanna?"

"I swear I'm telling you the truth."

"Truth about what?"

We turned. Phoebe stood in the doorway. I heard Zack gulp, and then he regained his composure.

"Oh, hi, Phoebe. Talking a little art with Madeline, that's all."

"Did I see my mother's car over here?" she asked.

He ran his hand nervously through his hair. "Yeah, she, uh, stopped by to talk to me about my show. You know, the one I told you about? The one she's setting up for me?"

"Oh, yes. How's that coming along?"

"Great, really great."

I was close enough to see Zack sweating, but Phoebe took him at his word.

"That makes me so happy. I told you she could do wonderful things for you."

Jerry turned his snort of laughter into a sneeze.

"Bless you," she said. "Zack, have you got time to come lift a washtub down off the wall for me?"

"Be right there."

She left, and Zack let his breath out in a gigantic sigh of relief. "Okay, as I said, I am telling you the truth about the museum robbery."

"But you could get in if you wanted to, right?" I asked.

"No, I couldn't!"

"Really? You never snuck into the museum?"

"I only did it one time, and then my mother found out and changed the lock," he said, his tone sullen. "One of the back doors near the loading dock."

"So you lied about that. Why were you sneaking in?"

"I did it to impress Wallie. Then she said she didn't like the idea. It wasn't like we were breaking the law or anything."

Actually, you were. "Wasn't there an alarm, or a camera?"

"Not if you know what codes to enter."

This squared with what Wallie had told me. "How did you know the codes?"

"I'd seen my mother do it." He folded his arms and attempted to look belligerent. "Are we done here?"

"For now," I said.

***

"Do you believe him?" Jerry asked as we drove away.

"Since he lied about getting into the museum, I'm not completely convinced," I said. "I'm still trying to reconcile that picture of him with Roxanna."

"A way to get back at his mom for not letting him sit at the big table?"

"He is, as Wallie said, fairly juvenile."

"Do you think Letticia knows?"

"I would say no, but then Roxanna strikes me as the type of person who'd want her to know."

"Are you thinking she had something to do with the break-in?"

"What does she stand to gain? I need to do some more investigating."

***

My investigation took a surprise turn when we got home and told Hayden about walking in on Roxanna and Zack Turner and the fact that Zack was having an affair with his girlfriend Phoebe's mother.

"That's unfortunate," he said. "I know Roxanna. She's one of my biggest supporters. She's arranged all my book signings and poetry readings."

This put a whole new slant on things. "How well do you know her?"

"She's a real patron of the arts, always willing to help new talent."

Well, that part was true.

"The big literary festival in Parkland last month was all her doing."

"Do you know anything about her daughter, Phoebe?" I asked.

"I don't believe I ever heard her mention a daughter."

"We're talking about the same person here? A tall, dark woman with a sharp nose and a domineering personality?"

"That's a good description."

"Could you find out about her relationship with Phoebe?" It was hard to believe spacey Phoebe had anything to do with the break-in, but I'd learned the hard way not to underestimate any possible suspect.

I wasn't sure if Hayden was mentally stable enough or even wanted to take part in a potentially awkward situation, but he brightened. "Help with the case? Of course! I could call her and say I wanted to set up another poetry reading."

"That might work."

"I know how I would feel if someone had stolen my poems—well, after my meltdown the other day, you know exactly how I'd react. I don't know how you're staying so calm."

I had a moment of doubt. "I don't want you to do this if you're not up to it."

"I've talked with Roxanna dozens of times. This won't be that different."

Jerry perched on the porch rail. "Make sure Hayden knows he doesn't have to literally go undercover with Mrs. Robinson."

"Oh, right," he said. "That can't end well."

"Be aware she likes younger men," I said.

Hayden grinned. "Don't worry, Madeline, I'll only take things so far."

I went upstairs to my studio, hoping to try out the little cloud creating brush stroke I'd learned from Tully. I hadn't painted two strokes before Mom called.

"Madeline, I don't know about lunch tomorrow."

She couldn't back out now. "Mom, everything will be all right. I think it will do you good to get out for a while."

"I feel so exposed. Unless you can find out who took those paintings, I am ruined socially."

I'd recently been on a case involving women to whom status meant everything. I didn't understand it then, and I didn't understand it now. "Mom, what's the worst thing that could happen? Maybe you lose a few friends. Were they real friends to begin with?"

"This is not about friends. This is about my standing in the arts community. We don't go to the movies or whatever it is you do with your girlfriends. We plan. We organize. We arrange."

"Why?"

"What do you mean?"

"Why do you do it? Is it fun?"

"I wouldn't exactly call it fun. It's satisfying."

"Mom, if you could do anything in the world, what would you do?"

She paused. "What kind of question is that?"

"Just answer it."

She took a long moment to reply. "Well, I've always wanted to travel."

News to me, but encouraging news. "Why don't you? You can afford it."

"I have too many responsibilities here."

I wanted to be flippant and say, not if I don't solve this case, but I didn't.

"Everything's going to work out."

My mother heaved a sigh that sounded exactly like mine at the end of a long day running around searching for clues. "I suppose."

"So you'll come to lunch?"

Another sigh. "All right. But if I don't like this friend of Jerry's, I'll suddenly have a headache, and you'd better take me home."

"It's a deal."

I worked until suppertime, had chicken and rice with the guys, and later, despite the rousing sounds of the Valkyries from Jerry's music room, found myself dozing off on the sofa. I woke when a wobbly soprano's voice declared something that sounded intensely serious, especially in German.

I slowly sat up and rearranged the cushions around me. "What's she so upset about?"

The lights were out except for the lamp on the end table. Hayden must have gone on to bed. Jerry sat down next to me. "Oh, she just found out her lover is actually her brother and that he has a mighty sword."

I started to laugh and couldn't stop. Jerry patted me on the back, feigning indignation. "Hey, this isn't funny. It's Wagner."

"What's she saying? I've got to know."

"Something along the lines of 'Art thou Siegmund, standing beside me? Sieglinda am I. You've won your sister as well as the sword.' See, there was this sword in a tree, and Siegmund was the only one who could pull it out."

This sent me into another round of giggles.

"Grow up. This is serious stuff. Then Siegmund sings, 'Bride and sister be to thy brother' just to seal the deal."

"Siegmund and Sieglinda? I thought somebody was named Siegfried."

"That would be their son."

"They had a baby? Eeeuww!" I fell over onto the sofa laughing.

Jerry waited until I'd caught my breath. "We could name our baby Siegfried."

"If we want him to spend his junior high school years squished in a locker, sure."

"We could call him Siggy. Siggy Fairweather."

"That sounds a bit precious." I sat up. "I dare you to tell my mother that's what we're going to name our son—if we ever have a boy."

He put his arm around me. "I will tell your mother anything. How about Fricka if it's a girl? Fricka Fairweather."

"Do I want to know where that came from?"

"It's a good old Wagnerian name. Fricka is Wotan's wife, and she rides around in a cart pulled by rams. Fricka Fairweather. Wow, I really like that."

My laughing spell had worn me out. "Okay, Fricka Fairweather it is. I'm too tired to fight you."

"If it's a boy, he can be Frick."

I didn't think I could laugh anymore, but I did. When I finally stopped, I remembered what my mother had told me. "Mom says if she doesn't like your friend, I have to take her home."

"Okay."

"She also admitted that she'd like to travel. I've never heard her mention that."

"I'll make sure she has a good time tomorrow."

"No cons, please."

"It's a little too late for that. She's going to have lunch with the Con Master." His gray eyes were at their most sincere. "I promise you, Mac. She'll be glad she did. You're glad you married me, aren't you?"

"We're not talking about Big Mike and my mother getting married."

Jerry's grin was impish. "We'll see."

CHAPTER THIRTEEN

I'd hoped to sleep a little later Sunday, but I was awakened by a chorus of little birds singing cheerfully to greet the morning. With a growl, I buried my head under my pillow, but once awake, all my worries began pushing and shoving to see who would be first in line.

Lunch with Mother and Big Mike. Another reason not to get up today. Sending Hayden off to spy on Roxanna. Maybe not the best idea. Doug Elmore and Zack Turner both had a good reason to see Letticia fail. Were there others out there gunning for her? Then there was Jake and Joanie—

Shut up and get up! I told myself. Nothing's too tough for Madeline Maclin, star of *From Crown to Crime!*

***

All morning and even right up until Jerry and I went by her house, I expected Mom to call and cancel, but she was waiting for us, dressed in an elegant black suit. All the way to the Elms, she quizzed Jerry about Michael Crown. Jerry had a good time making up all sorts of stories about his former boss, stories I hoped Big Mike could confirm.

The restaurant wasn't full, and our table was in a corner, sheltered by ornamental trees and a fancy screen, but this didn't keep Mom from hiding her face with her purse as we walked to our seats. I tried to lighten the mood by telling her people would mistake her for a rock star. She glared and took a chair at the far end of the table. Jerry told the waiter there was one more member in our party and that we'd wait for him.

We didn't have to wait long before Big Mike made his entrance.

I would think twice before crossing someone as large and imposing as Big Mike. He was dressed in an obviously expensive suit and a silk tie, all in muted shades of brown. He gave a nod to the maître d', who signaled two waiters to bring an oversized chair to our table. Jerry stood to shake Big Mike's hand, barely reaching the older man's shoulder.

"Mr. Crown, thanks for coming."

"My pleasure." He grinned at Jerry's tie with its pattern of little black and white dice, acknowledging the reference to the crown and anchor game.

Nicely played, I thought.

"You know Madeline, of course, and this is her mother, Cecille Maclin."

Big Mike shook Mom's hand and gave a little bow. "Charmed."

Mom was indeed charmed. "Mr. Crown."

"Michael, please."

Mom was impressed, but who wouldn't be? Big Mike's wide, pleasantly bland face, well-cut clothes, and assured air screamed wealth and importance, two things she admired. One waiter handed Big Mike a menu and stood at attention while another took our drink orders. After we'd made our selections and drinks had been served, Jerry clued Big Mike in to the background he'd created.

"I was telling Cecille about your overseas holdings, the computer business, and all the libraries you support."

Big Mike didn't hesitate. "Yes, I have several companies overseas. One in Paris, one in London, and one in Berlin. I spend a lot of time traveling to keep an eye on things. Do you enjoy traveling, Cecille?"

The mention of Paris and London brought a sparkle to Mom's eyes. "It has been a dream of mine to travel."

"I imagine your work here in the city keeps you too busy."

"Well, I do hold some important positions. There's been some trouble at the art museum, but Madeline is taking care of that."

Big Mike grinned. "I've heard good things about Madeline and her agency."

All through lunch, Big Mike kept us entertained with tales about his travels. Mom did not get a headache. Often, I exchanged a glance with Jerry that expressed my wonder at my mother's behavior. I couldn't believe the relaxed and pleasant woman sitting beside me chatting away as if she'd known Big Mike for years was the same overly anxious woman who'd been afraid to go out in public. Of course, he appeared to be completely interested in what she had to say, and credit had to go to Jerry's clever manipulation, mentioning appealing overseas connections when he knew Mom had expressed a desire to travel. I would've been comfortable to sit back and let the two men work their magic, but part of me worried that this might all be for show. Still, Mom was out of the house and having a good time.

Before dessert, Mom excused herself to go to the ladies room. When she got up, Big Mike and Jerry stood, which pleased her.

Big Mike sat down and picked up the dessert menu. "Your mother is a delightful woman, Madeline. Thank you for introducing us."

"Thank you for entertaining her. She's been very upset about what happened at the museum. This was the very thing."

"Glad I could help. You won't object, then, if I call on her again?"

What could I say? My mother was a grown woman, and if she didn't want to see Big Mike, she'd say so. But I had to make sure of one thing. "She really does want to travel. What you said about your overseas companies—is that true?"

He chuckled. "Yes. They aren't your typical companies, but they are in Europe, and I do check on them from time to time. Anything else you want to know?"

I knew better than to ask about Sobbin' Susie. Even if I had questions, this wasn't the time or the place to discuss a takeover attempt. "I don't believe so."

"Now, what do you like? Chocolate Fantasy Cake with ice cream and almonds or Dazzling Peach Cobbler? Both sound delicious."

Mom returned looking flustered. "I had a close call in the ladies room. I heard Prissy Troxler talking to someone, and I had to wait until they left before I came out to wash my hands."

Big Mike's voice held an undercurrent of serious intent. "Is this woman a problem?"

"Oh, no," I said. "She's a friend of Mother's, but Mom would rather not talk to her right now. She's also on the museum board."

"Surely no one blames you for the crime, Cecille."

"The gala was my responsibility," she said.

"But you couldn't have foreseen such an incident."

"I still feel terrible about it."

"Madeline will take care of everything." He signaled for the waiter. "Now, we're all having Chocolate Fantasy Cake and Dazzling Peach Cobbler. Lots of dessert and no more talking about the museum." He gave me a wink. "Or anything else job related."

That's what we did. Big Mike charmed Mom back into a good mood. He insisted on paying for lunch, said he hoped he could see her again, and made a grand exit.

As we drove Mom back to her house, she said, "Jerry, I have to say your friend was not what I expected. How did you two meet? He wouldn't have been in college with you."

"I met him after I graduated. I worked for him a while."

Mom knew Jerry had given up any claim to the Fairweather fortune. "That makes sense. You needed a job, and he has all these companies. What were you in? Sales?"

"In a way. Michael taught me all the tricks of the trade."

"He's a very nice man. Very well to do, I see."

"I imagine he could keep you in the way to which you are accustomed."

Mom pretended to be offended, but couldn't suppress a smile. "You're getting ahead of yourself."

***

After we dropped Mom off at her house, I stared at my husband. "Good grief, she actually joked with you."

"See what a little Chocolate Fantasy can do?"

"Seriously, Jerry. What are Big Mike's intentions? Should I be as worried as I am?"

"First of all, there's no way to stop him, so play along. Second, he's always been a gentleman when it comes to the ladies. And third, he genuinely likes your mother. I think we should let it unfold."

"Or unravel."

We had an hour before Amanda's reception at First Baptist Church. I parked near a little hot dog restaurant and called Hayden to see if he'd found out anything from Roxanna.

"It's very odd, Madeline," he said. "I told her I'd recently learned she had a daughter who was an artist, and her manner changed immediately. She said she and Phoebe were estranged and she didn't want to talk about her. Then she talked about her for a good ten minutes. She said she'd done everything she could for her, but Phoebe didn't appreciate it. She'd paid for Phoebe's education, and Phoebe dropped out of school. She tried to get Phoebe jobs, but Phoebe always quit. Plus no matter how many times Roxanna told her, Phoebe refused to believe she had no artistic talent. When she stopped for breath, I apologized, and we continued to talk about my poetry and what I was working on."

"Wow, so no mother/daughter banquet plans there. When I talked with Roxanna, she was just as negative. She called Phoebe's art trash and told me Phoebe wouldn't have the brains or the energy to pull off a crime."

"That's harsh."

Unless Phoebe knew about her mother and Zack. That could be enough to set her into action. "Sorry she unloaded on you."

"Can you imagine having a mother like that? Poor Phoebe."

"Did Roxanna say anything about the museum?"

"She told me how careless Letticia had been lately, but that was it. She mainly wanted to talk about the exhibit she's created. Oh, and Shana called. Her tour is going well, and she said to thank you again for letting me bunk at your place."

"No problem. Where are you now?"

"On your porch."

"We'll see you after a while."

I relayed all Hayden's information to Jerry, and as we set off for First Baptist to congratulate the happy couple, I had a call from Jake. "Where are you now, Madeline? What's the latest?"

I could truthfully tell him I was on my way to a wedding reception.

Jake's voice was full of disbelief. "Really? Isn't your case—well, I don't want to tell you how to run your investigation, but isn't the museum case more important?"

"You remember Joanie Raines and her complaint about Amanda Price? I've got to take care of that, too."

There was a return of his enthusiasm. "Want me to dig up dirt on Amanda?"

"No, I already know what kind of person she is. You're welcome to come to the reception."

"Sounds like fun," he said, "but it's raining spiders on Fifth Street."

"Seriously?" I said.

I heard the grin in his voice. "Well, no, but the *Galaxy* will make it so. I'll check with you later."

***

The reception hall looked as if a bridal show had decided to display all of its latest in over the top decorations. Swaths of white tulle filled with little twinkly lights, pink flowers, and tiny mechanical blue birds chirping away hung over the crowd like fantasy clouds. Masses of red roses loomed out of crystal vases and dripped with more of the little blinking lights. The main table sat on a raised platform outlined in red roses and lights. The chairs were adorned with huge heart-shaped cut outs. These were also blinking.

Jerry was impressed. "Welcome to Vegas."

If Amanda Price was surprised to see us, she was too much in control to show it. She swooped down on us in an array of pink ruffles and a large hat complete with feathers and a diamond pin. "Well, isn't this nice!" She motioned to her new husband. "Anderson, this is Madeline Maclin and her husband, Jerry Fairweather.

They came all the way over from Celosia. Madeline and Jerry, this is my husband, Anderson Stratton."

Stratton was a tall man with white hair and a beard and gold-rimmed glasses. He looked like a scientist ready to lecture on negative particles in the atmosphere. We shook hands all around and made small talk until Stratton was called off to another group of well-wishers.

Amanda turned to me. Maybe I should say Amanda turned on me. "What in the world are you doing here?"

"Joanie Raines seems to think you have something that belongs to the Rossboro Arts Council."

"What on earth would that be?"

"Five thousand dollars."

Amanda's face became as pink as her outfit. "The nerve of that woman! She'll do anything to discredit me! Why would she think I took their piddling little five thousand dollars? I'm marrying a millionaire!"

"Oh?"

She looked smug. "Apparently, you didn't know that Anderson is very wealthy. In fact, he's going to finance my own production of Emmaline's story."

I didn't dare look at Jerry. *Three* outdoor dramas about Emmaline Ross? "That's great, Amanda. I'm very happy for you, and congratulations to you and Anderson."

"And our deepest sympathies to the groom," Jerry said so only I could hear.

Amanda was so caught up in her overblown festivities she wouldn't have heard him, anyway. "Isn't this the most amazing cake? Anderson had his own French chef flown in from Paris. The dew drops on the candied roses are real diamonds, by the way. The decorations are by Emilio, who is the most exclusive designer in the world. He's impossible to get. Oh, there's the mayor's wife. I must speak with her. You can show yourselves out, can't you? Excuse me."

We were ready to show ourselves out. "It amazes me that people like Amanda always land on their feet," I said as we exited the church fellowship hall.

Jerry agreed. "I could take lessons from her. But why would she steal money from Rossboro when she's marrying a man wealthy enough to finance her next vanity project?"

"To undermine the Rossboro production?" I took out my phone and called Joanie. "Amanda just married another millionaire," I told her.

"What?" Joanie spluttered. "She's married again?"

"Yes, so she doesn't need money. Who else might have taken it?"

"No one! It has to be Amanda!"

"No, you want it to be Amanda. There's a difference. Keep looking. Jerry and I will be back to Rossboro sometime today."

My phone rang, and when I saw Mom's name on the caller ID, I entertained the thought that she and Big Mike had eloped and were on their way to Paris. I thought she was anxious for news about the paintings, but she was more interested in her lunch date.

"Madeline, tell Jerry again I certainly enjoyed meeting his friend. Such an interesting man. Obviously from old money like the Fairweathers. I'm glad Jerry's decided to make those connections."

"Yes, he's very good at making connections."

"All right, then. See you later."

No heartfelt sigh? No laying on of guilt? My mother sounded like a regular, cheerful person. I must have stared at the phone for longer than I thought because Jerry had to say my name several times.

"Sorry. My mother had a human moment."

My next call was from Letticia. It was not as heartening as my mother's.

"Doug Elmore has called a board meeting for tomorrow," she said. "You know what's going to be number one on the agenda."

"I know there are board members who support you," I said.

"Yes, but all of this is so discouraging."

"Don't give up yet," I said. "I'm doing all I can."

"I know, Madeline, and believe me, I appreciate it."

That was all I could tell her. She thanked me and ended the call.

"What would you like to do now?" Jerry asked.

"I want answers now. I am just about to split."

Jerry spared me a sympathetic glance. "That's because right now, you're Mood Swing Mac, which is why I'm driving."

I was still grumbling to myself when Jerry and I got back in the car. As he turned back toward Celosia, he took a different street.

"Where are you going?" I asked.

"I thought we'd stop in and say hi to Tucker."

I was surprised that Jerry wanted to go by his family home. In the past, he didn't want to have anything to do with the house, but since I'd discovered he was not responsible for the fire that had killed his parents, he was beginning to feel more at ease visiting his younger brother.

I had been to the Fairweather mansion only once, and that was for Tucker's wedding. The house was located in a part of Parkland so upscale I hadn't known the area existed, a stunning mansion made entirely of yellow brick and white stone. It gleamed golden in the sunlight. A curved drive lined with trees led up to the porch, which was supported by white columns and decorated with huge stone vases spilling over with purple flowers that made a dramatic contrast against the yellow brick.

Jerry and I walked around the house to the garden, but I remembered how magnificent everything was inside, a foyer floor of gold and white stones, a double staircase sweeping up into golden rooms. I'd had a look at the surprisingly modern living room with its low slung couches, oddly-shaped tables, and touches of chrome, and the dining room, furnished with a long cherry wood table and chairs with elaborately curved backs and arms. It was in the living room that I'd seen the portrait of the three Fairweather boys as children, older, darker Des standing with his hand on Jerry's shoulder, and Jerry sitting with baby Tucker in his lap. The boys had a sister, but she wasn't in the portrait, something that had caused more than a rift in the family, a rift now mended, thanks in part to my solving the mystery of their parents' death.

Present-day Tucker was a shorter version of Jerry, the same light brown hair, the same gray eyes. Since neither Des nor Jerry wanted to live in the house, Tucker had been happy to take over. He was a gardener, and his roses were the pride of the vast gardens behind the Fairweather estate. The different varieties and colors of roses had names like "Peace" and "Special Occasion," "Bewitched" and "Awareness," and some were named for people and celebrities like "Judy Garland" and "Mister Lincoln." Tucker had also planted a lavender rose called "Blue Moon" in honor of my most successful painting and enjoyed teasing me about the golden one named "Royal Pageant."

The garden spread out all the way to private woodland, smooth green lawns, bushes cut into fanciful shapes, statues, even a maze. A fountain with leaping stone dolphins dominated the center of the garden. We found Tucker knee deep in iris he was pulling from a bed around a statue of a mother reading to a child. He peeled off his muddy gloves and he and Jerry hugged and slapped each other on the back. Then he gave me a hug.

"Good to see you! What brings you out this way?"

"We were in town and thought we'd stop by. Where's Selene?"

"She's visiting her father today. She should be back soon."

His wife Selene was the most ethereal looking young woman I'd ever seen. She looked as if she'd just stepped into our world from a fairy tale. The garden was the perfect setting for her.

Tucker wiped his hands on his worn jeans. "Good timing, guys. I'm ready for a break. Let's sit on the porch and have a drink."

While our porch was comfortably rustic with a grand total of four used rocking chairs, Tucker's porch was as big as our living room and looked out over an equally large terrace of yellow brick. The yellow wicker furniture had flowered cushions, the glass tables were trimmed in brass, and huge baskets filled with purple and white striped petunias sat on the polished wood floor. A mild breeze ruffled the edges of the gardening magazines on the center table. The magazines were held in place by brass paperweights shaped like flowers.

I sat down in a chair and Jerry took the sofa. Tucker said he'd be right back and disappeared into the house.

I couldn't imagine Selene doing housework. "This place always looks immaculate. Does Tucker hire an army to keep it up?"

"I don't know how he does it, but he's got plenty of money to pay a cleaning service."

"He does all the gardening himself, though."

"Oh, yes. He won't let anyone else mess with it."

Tucker returned with a tray carrying three glasses of tea and a plate of cookies, which he set down on the center table. He handed me a glass and passed the cookies.

"Selene made these yesterday."

Jerry took a glass. "She cooks, too?"

"She does everything. She's magic."

"I believe you."

Tucker took the remaining glass and sat down in one of the flowered chairs.

"How are you getting along, Madeline? Are you working on a case now?"

"Did you hear about the Parkland Museum of Art being robbed? The director hired me."

Jerry reached for a cookie. "Unfortunately, one of the paintings that was stolen was *Blue Moon Garden*."

"Oh, no."

I took a sip of tea and set my glass aside. "It's like that old line from the movies. This time, it's personal."

"I wish there was something I could do to help," Tucker said, "but I'm out in the garden all the time. It's my own world out there. I rarely know what's happening anywhere else."

"That's okay," I said. "It's really nice just to sit here in this beautiful place and not think about it for a while." My shoulders were no longer up around my ears, and my intense desire to strangle someone had abated. I realized that was why Jerry wanted to stop by his family home. The garden really was another world, a peaceful world filled with light and color, an inspiring world. Looking around, I saw dozens of scenes I wanted to paint.

"You know you're welcome here anytime," Tucker said.

"Thanks. I may have to recreate *Blue Moon Garden*, but I see a lot of other things that are calling out to me, including another cookie. These are delicious."

"Eat all you want." Tucker chatted on about the types of roses he was planning to cultivate, the flower show he wanted to attend, and his own hybrid rose he was attempting to grow. "I thought

I would call it Lillian, after our mother," he told Jerry. "There's already a 'Lilian Austin,' pink shaded with orange and apricot, but my rose would be white with touches of gold."

"That sounds nice," Jerry said.

I sat back and listened as Tucker talked about floribunda roses named "Angel Face" and "Iceberg," a miniature rose called "Rainbow's End," hybrid tea roses with beautiful names, "Keepsake," "Paradise," and "Fragrant Cloud."

"Those are some of the most fragrant roses. I like to use 'Fourth of July' on the pergola. I have to take the old wood off the roses after they flower and train the new wood. That way the walkway isn't covered with little shoots."

Tucker could go on for hours about his garden, and when he got into proper forms of pruning, Jerry leaned over and gave him a friendly punch on the shoulder. "Time out. Mac's eyes are glazing over."

As Tucker started to apologize, I held up a hand. "No, no. It's all very soothing. A lot better than questioning suspects and worrying about my painting."

"Can you stay for dinner? I promise no more rose talk."

As much as I wanted to stay on this golden porch surrounded by flowers and lulled by the conversation of nitrogen versus potassium deficiency, I needed to get home.

"Thank you, but we should be going. Tell Selene we're sorry we missed her."

Once in the car, I gave Jerry a kiss. "And thank you for this much needed break."

CHAPTER FOURTEEN

The sight of our house looked calm and welcoming, the late afternoon sun reflecting in the windows. Hayden was on the porch with Denisha, and Austin's four-wheeler was parked under a tree. Everything looked safe and not stupid. I took a deep breath.

"You okay?" Jerry asked, as he pulled in beside the four-wheeler.

"Better."

We got out, and Austin galloped up. "Jerry! Want to go to the haunted house? We should get there before dark. How 'bout you, Madeline? Denisha and Hayden don't want to go."

"No, thanks. You two check it out first."

Austin was so eager to see the haunted house he tossed Jerry the spare helmet and leaped onto the four-wheeler. Jerry hopped on behind and they roared off across the meadow.

Denisha handed me her notebook. "I've written five more poems, Madeline, and Hayden has written another one, and I'm going to illustrate them. Hayden's going to show me how to make a cover, too. He's really helpful."

No, you're the helpful one, I thought. *You've been the perfect thing to keep him occupied.* "Are you going to make copies of this poetry book for everyone?"

"Yes, and I'm going to have my own signing party. Hayden said he would talk to Georgia at the bookstore and set everything up."

"That sounds exciting."

"Much more exciting than a stupid haunted house," she said, and Hayden agreed.

I wanted to hear more about this venture, but my phone rang. It was Joanie Raines. "Excuse me. I have to take this call."

I had completely forgotten I'd told Joanie that Jerry and I would come back to Rossboro, so she was understandably aggrieved.

"Madeline, I'm counting on you to solve this."

"I'm sorry. There's been a lot going on today." Lunch with Big Mike, Amanda's reception, a stalled investigation. If I hadn't had my Fairweather garden break, I would have been screaming with frustration. "We'll come over tomorrow."

"Doesn't it seem suspicious to you that Amanda would pack up suddenly and leave town and marry someone out of the blue like that?"

"No, having dealt with Amanda, this sounds like reasonable behavior for her."

"She would've been bragging about marrying a millionaire for weeks. This is a plot, I know it is."

I decided not to bring up the third Emmaline Ross drama Amanda was planning to have her new husband finance. "Joanie, I promise, I'll see you tomorrow, and we'll figure this out."

Joanie huffed and puffed for a few more moments and grudgingly agreed.

The boys came back in about an hour, and Austin reported that the house wasn't nearly as scary as advertised.

"I thought there'd be bones lying around or something. It's just rundown, like your house used to be, only worse. But we saw a rat, didn't we, Jerry? A whopping big one with red eyes. I'll bet there's a whole pack of them living under the house."

"Did you go inside?" I asked.

"We got as far as the front door before part of the roof fell in," Jerry said. "We decided it might not be safe."

"Yeah, we didn't want to fall through to the zombies' underground hideout. We looked in the windows, but it was too dark to see if the walls were bleeding."

"Eeeuww," Denisha said. "Why would they be bleeding?"

Austin rolled his eyes. "Duh, because of the zombies. We can go back another time, can't we, Jerry?"

Jerry assured him they would. "First let me find a couple of hard hats."

Austin patted his stomach. "Man, all that with the rats and everything made me hungry. What are you guys having for supper?"

***

That night I dreamed I was running along a highway that zigged and zagged and turned me upside down. It was like trying to run on a Mobius strip. Each time I arrived at a destination, I was either too late or too early for whatever was supposed to happen. Paintings floated past me, but I couldn't catch one. The paintings were of clowns wearing sashes and tiaras. They pageant-waved as they sailed by. Then Jake was there with an old-fashioned movie camera. "There's not enough drama," he kept shouting. "I need more action!" The dream shifted and now someone had smashed all my paintings and thrown them into Phoebe's fish pond. When I tried to pull them out, my hands, which had tattoos all over them like Rusty's, got tangled in something I couldn't see. Big Mike appeared. "Don't worry, Madeline," he said. "I'll get you out. But you'll owe me another favor." "No, no, I can get it," I said. I gave one more desperate yank, and everything came up and crashed over me.

I woke with a start. Jerry made a grumpy sound and turned over. I knew I couldn't get back to sleep right away after all that, so I stumbled down to the kitchen for something to eat. When I saw a man in the kitchen, I stopped dead still. For a few distracted moments, I thought I was still dreaming. Wasn't I in bed with Jerry? Then what was he doing in the kitchen?

"Jerry?"

The man turned, and I saw it was Hayden. "Oh, hi, Madeline. Sorry if I startled you. I couldn't sleep and thought I'd get a snack."

His height and size had fooled me. "I thought Jerry had done the best trick of his life."

"What can I get for you?"

"Some milk and crackers oughta do the trick."

"I'm having leftover bacon and peanut butter."

"That sounds good, too." I got a glass of milk and brought it and the box of crackers to the table. We sat down to eat our snacks. "I'm glad you didn't feel the urge to wander the fields tonight."

"No, sometimes my medicine makes me hungry, that's all." He took a bite of his odd combination and pushed the peanut butter jar across the table toward me. "I'm feeling so much better. I'd like to say it's the quiet or the fresh country air, but I think it's the not sitting around thinking about myself all day. I was very lucky to have my mother for as long as I did. Talking with Denisha, I realized I was very lucky to have a mother, at all. How's your mother doing?"

"She's still worried about her social status, but she's calmed down some."

"What about your father, if you don't mind me asking?"

"My parents divorced soon after I was born, and he died a few years later. She never says a word about him."

"So no pictures? No happy memories?"

I dipped a cracker into my milk. "I don't want you to think my life was tragic. Mom did a great job looking after me, it's just that her idea of looking out meant hauling me around to Little Miss Pageants whenever possible. Maybe her marriage couldn't be perfect, but she was bound and determined her child would be." I reached for the peanut butter and the knife. "I'd like to be happier for her but Big Mike worries me. Mom only likes men she can control."

Hayden smiled. "You think his intentions aren't honorable?"

I made two peanut butter crackers. "Who knows? He's a law and country unto himself."

"Jerry told me a little about him. What does he look like?"

"You remember Rusty, my biggest fan? Well, imagine if Rusty was about a foot taller and several feet wider, extremely wealthy, and didn't have all the tattoos."

Hayden was impressed. "I would run the other way."

We ate for a few more minutes. I had two slices of bacon, dunked one more cracker, and drank the milk. Hayden finished the last of the bacon and put the lid back on the peanut butter jar.

"Thanks for letting me help on the case, Madeline. It's a good distraction."

"You're welcome. I need all the help I can get on this one."

"Roxanna said something about a board meeting tomorrow. I'll see if I can sit in. Maybe I could learn something useful."

"She doesn't know you're staying here, does she?"

"No, I haven't said anything about that."

I recalled that Hayden's imagination had caused Shana and me some concern when he wandered off into the forest one night, convinced he'd seen a ghost and needed to do her bidding. "You're enjoying this way too much, but don't get carried away."

Hayden promised to be careful, and he and I went back to our beds. Jerry rolled over and squinted at me. "You all right?"

I snuggled in. "Needed a snack."

"You smell like bacon. You're my perfect woman."

Curled up close to him, I found it easy to go to sleep. Thank goodness I didn't have any more dreams.

***

Monday morning, Jerry went off to breakfast duty at Deely's, Hayden drove off in his Mini Cooper to Parkland to meet with Roxanna, and I called Joanie.

"Checking in as promised," I said.

Joanie fired right in. "Just because Amanda says she didn't steal that money doesn't mean she didn't."

"Not even if she's married a millionaire?"

"That doesn't matter. She could've taken that money out of spite. We need to file a formal complaint with the Rossboro Arts Council."

"Joanie," I said as patiently as I could, "I've been running back and forth to Rossboro for days now. You live in Celosia. I live in Celosia. I'll come by your house."

"That's not really necessary, Madeline."

"Your house. Ten minutes. See you there."

***

I'd been to Joanie's house before. I remembered all the pink ruffles from the welcome mat to the wreath on the front door. Even the rocking chair on the porch had pink ruffled cushions, and a large ceramic duck sat on the top step holding a basket of pink flowers decorated with a ruffly pink bow.

Joanie answered the door and stood in the doorway. "I don't know why you wanted to meet here," she said. "We should be at the Rossboro Arts Council."

Now I was curious. Joanie was extremely proud of her house and loved showing it off. "May I use your bathroom?" I asked. "One too many cups of coffee this morning."

She grudgingly stepped aside for me to enter the narrow foyer. I walked down the hallway to the bathroom, being careful not to dislodge any of the decorative plates hanging on the walls. After a quick pretend trip to the bathroom, I came out and peeked into the living room, a small pink room with a pink flowered sofa. "Oh, you've got some new rabbits."

Large white ceramic rabbits sat in the corners of the living room, lounged on the window ledge, and peered down from the bookshelf. All were wearing pink ribbons. I wandered in for a closer look.

Joanie followed me. She tugged at her ponytail and clasped her hands together. "Not exactly new."

Ordinarily, I would be subjected to each rabbit's history, where she bought it, how much it cost, how well it matched all the others, but Joanie watched me anxiously, as if I might suddenly snatch up a rabbit and toss it out the window. By now, I was certain Joanie wanted me out of her house, and I could think of one good reason why. So I strolled around admiring every little knickknack on every little table. When I reached the bookshelf, I saw her eyes dart to a book that was sticking out a little further from its neighbors. She gave her ponytail another nervous tug. I'd been around Jerry and his friends long enough to know what a "tell" was.

I pulled the book from the shelf. "This looks interesting. *The Collector's Guide to Ceramic Figures.*" I flipped through the pages and found an envelope. "You've left something in here. A bookmark, maybe?"

Joanie, red-faced and stammering, said it wasn't a bookmark.

I set the book aside and opened the envelope. "This wouldn't happen to be five thousand dollars that belongs to the Rossboro Little Theater, would it?"

"I wasn't going to keep it!"

I could feel Mood Mac rising to the surface and pushed her down. I spoke calmly. "You just wanted Amanda to be blamed."

Joanie plopped into one of the chairs and buried her face in her hands. "She gets away with everything! She deserved to know what it feels like when somebody else makes trouble for *her*. Just once." She gave a huge sigh and lifted her face. Her eyes were filled with tears. "I planned to pretend to find it, and give it back. Eventually."

"You're not a very good liar, Joanie."

"I know, I know." Another sigh. "I guess you have to call the police."

"Take the money back to the Arts Council and explain everything," I said. "It's up to them if they want to press charges."

She nodded and wiped her face. "Sorry I caused you so much trouble, Madeline."

"That's okay," I said. "But all this hatred is what caused the trouble. You need to get that under control." I felt a sudden rush of sympathy. *Like my bad moods*, I thought. *Here's a lesson for you, Madeline.*

***

After downing another large cup of coffee and a bacon and egg biscuit at Deely's, I felt more in control. I sat back in my booth and listened to the conversations flowing around me, mingled with the good smells of bacon, waffles, and coffee. Control. Yes, that's what was lacking recently. I had vowed to lighten up on my intense desire to control the world, but these mood attacks weren't making it easy.

Jerry came over to the booth, two fingers held up like a cross to keep vampires at bay. "Is it safe to approach?"

"Only if you'll bring me a pickle."

He returned with the giant industrial jar and set it on the table. "You might need more than one." He unscrewed the lid and sat down across from me. "So what's up?"

"Guess who took the five thousand dollars from the Rossboro Little Theater? Not the evil Amanda, but the ever so hate-filled Joanie Raines."

"Now there's a plot for a mystery," he said. "Bitter Actress Frames Hated Rival. Did she confess to the crime?"

"After I found the money in her house."

"I'm surprised you could find it in amongst all the rabbits. So, case closed, right?"

"Until the next loony thing happens with all these dramas." I attempted to pry a pickle from the jar.

Jerry indicated the jar. "You need some help with that?"

"Let me take out my aggressions on the pickles. It's safer. Hayden hasn't called you, has he?"

"No, but we've been super busy this morning."

"I told him we'd meet him in Parkland." I finally succeeded in prying a pickle from the pack. "Mom hasn't called, either, which I guess is a good thing."

"She and Big Mike are half way to Vegas." I must have looked alarmed for a second because Jerry laughed and said, "Just kidding. He did say he was going to call on her again, didn't he?"

"Yes, and she could say no. She probably will, now that she's had time to think about it."

Jerry was called back to the kitchen. I found it ironic that after all my moaning about Mom's frequent calls I wanted to hear from her. I munched on my pickle, wondering if I should check on her, but decided not to go down that road. Then I worried about Hayden. Was he slinking along the corridors of the museum, hunting for clues? It would be just like him to go overboard on his plan to infiltrate the board. When I couldn't stand it anymore, I called him.

He sounded perfectly fine. "Oh, hi, Madeline. I told Roxanna I was interested in joining the museum board, and they meet today at eleven, so I'm hanging out at Between the Covers till then."

Between the Covers was an upscale book and coffee shop in Parkland. "Okay, Jerry and I will meet you there."

"I did find out something that might be useful, though. Wait a second." I heard a door open and close and the sounds of traffic. "I stepped outside to talk. There was an article in the *Parkland Herald* today about the museum. It said the museum was having financial trouble and may have to downsize. The gala was supposed to have been a big fund raiser, and with that not happening, things look to be going further downhill. According to the paper, nobody's job is safe, not even the director's. I'll bet they'll discuss that in their next meeting."

"You're right, and if you can get into that part of the meeting, that would be very helpful. See you soon."

CHAPTER FIFTEEN

Between the Covers in Parkland was located between a dress shop and a shop that as far as I could see sold only incredibly expensive paperweights. Hayden was seated in one of the secluded areas the book store had for its patrons, a circle of leather chairs surrounded by bookshelves filled with the latest best sellers and paperbacks by local authors. Hayden's poetry collection, *Glass Plums*, was prominently displayed, as well as the latest issue of *Artistic Review*. I didn't realize the magazine was still around. *Artistic Review* had been on the scene when I first started painting. At that time, I'd been too lowly to rate a review from them.

"Here's the newspaper article I was talking about, Madeline," Hayden said.

He spread the morning edition of the *Parkland Herald* out on the low round table. I read the article and passed the paper to Jerry. "Mom's not going to be happy her name is front and center with the other board members."

"See anyone else who might be the mastermind behind the break-in?" he asked.

"That's where super spy Hayden Amry comes in."

Jerry grinned at his friend. "Have you accepted this mission?"

"I'm ready."

I folded the paper and put it back on the table. "You shouldn't have any problem in the meeting, but do what Jerry always tells me and make sure you know where at least two exits are."

"I plan to sit quietly and listen and maybe nod every now and then." He checked his watch. "I'd better head over there."

"All right," I said. "Call me after the meeting and we'll compare notes."

***

I bought the copy of *Artistic Review*. I was curious to see if the magazine had changed over the years. The reviews were still written in a snooty style filled with unnecessarily big words, and the news from the art world was concerned with gallery openings, up and coming artists, and the outrageous prices people paid for art work at prestigious auction houses.

I closed the magazine. "I'm still not worthy."

"Would a mention in there help your career?"

"Maybe."

"Who runs the magazine?"

I opened *Artistic Review* and near the front found the list of names. "No one I recognize—hold on, I'd forgotten that one of the contributing editors was Letticia. I wonder..."

I wondered long enough for Jerry to ask, "Wonder what?"

"If Roxanna was ever asked to contribute." I got out my phone. "There's probably an archive I can check."

Sure enough, there was. I typed in Roxanna Deluca. A few moments later, I found her. But she wasn't and hadn't been an editor. What I found was a review of her work, written by Letticia Booth. "Uh, oh."

"What is it?"

"A not so good review written by Letticia. 'Deluca has a tendency towards jittery execution and shows no aptitude for negative space.'"

"Ouch."

"'However, she does make good use of *trompe l'oeil* and her subject matter, though trite, is given a fresh rendering.' A fancy way of saying her work is not quite but almost crap."

"*Trompe l'oeil?* I've heard of that. It's some kind of optical illusion, right?"

"Yes, it's artwork that creates the illusion of a three-dimensional object."

"But Roxanna's was trite yet fresh. She was probably not happy with that assessment."

"And that's one more reason she has to hate Letticia."

***

We stopped by a little hot dog restaurant to get some lunch and to wait on Hayden's report. It wasn't long before he called. The board had gone into private session, and he was in the museum coffee shop.

"Everyone welcomed me, but I haven't been officially approved as a new member, so after a brief discussion of the agenda, I wasn't allowed to stay," he said. "I can ask Roxanna afterwards how the meeting went, but one of the items on the agenda was a performance review of the museum director."

"Did they have enough members there to hold a vote?" I asked.

"I asked Roxanna how many members were needed for a quorum. She said out of the fourteen members, they'd need ten there. I counted eight."

"Letticia has been granted a reprieve," I said. "See what Roxanna says. I imagine it'll take more than one meeting to decide something this serious."

"Okay," he said. "What else would you like me to do?"

He sounded so eager I didn't have the heart to tell him I wanted him to go home and stay out of trouble. I checked my watch. "The kids'll be stopping by the house soon. Weren't you going to help Denisha put her poetry book together?"

To my relief, he agreed. "That's right. After I talk with Roxanna, I'll head back to the house. Call me if you need any more help."

"Hayden's all set," I said to Jerry. "Let me give Jake a call." I punched in Jake's number. "This is going to sound crazy, but I almost miss having him around. It's hard to hold out against such relentless enthusiasm. Jake's married, right? What does his wife think about supernatural stuff?"

"I believe a strange supernatural event brought them together."

I wanted to hear about that, but Jake answered. "Sorry I missed you! I was heading your way when a two-headed snake got loose in the *Galaxy* office, and I was the only one who could catch it. Everybody else leaped up on their desks and screamed like it was the end of the world. You see why I want a better job? What did you find out?"

I filled Jake in on the day's activities and told him to meet us at Zack's studio in an hour I could almost see his high powered grin through the phone.

"Excellent!" he said. "I will definitely be there, and no two-headed snake will deter me."

***

We were halfway down the narrow dirt road to Applestone when another car passed us in a cloud of dust. I had to swerve to avoid being side-swiped. I caught a glimpse of silver, but the driver was going too fast for me to see a face.

"Somebody's in a hurry," I remarked. "Was that Roxanna's car?"

Jerry turned in his seat to get a better look. "All I can see is dust."

Zack was outside his studio, hacking away on a large chunk of granite. He stopped working and pushed his safety glasses up into his hair. He regarded us warily. "Hi, guys." He was further disconcerted by the sight of Jake's Gremlin wheeling into the driveway. Jake hopped out and gave him a cheerful wave.

"Hi," I said. "Mind if I ask you a few more questions?"

"Fire away. Oh, and thanks again for not saying anything to Phoebe about, you know."

That didn't mean I wouldn't bring up Zack's affair if I needed to, but right now, that was between him and his conscience. "Was Roxanna just here? Jerry and I saw a silver car as we came in."

"No. Must have been someone else's car." Zack gestured to Jake. "Why is he filming this? What's going on?"

But before I could answer, the wind brought a sudden smell of smoke and burning metal.

"Oh, my God!" Zack pointed toward a column of thick gray

smoke. "Phoebe's studio!"

We all punched in nine-one-one as we ran for the studio. Zack got there first.

"Phoebe!"

He rushed into the smoke-filled maze of wire, pipes, and junk. Jerry grabbed him and yanked him back as a wall of flame went up in a whoosh of heat and sparks. Phoebe's piles of found art crackled and popped, fiery bits of paper swirling in the smoke.

"We can't get in that way. Try the back!"

Zack ran one way and Jerry and I ran another, circling the fire, searching for a glimpse of Phoebe. Behind her studio, the pieces twisted and melted as the flames danced across the roof. I was imagining the worst when I saw Phoebe. Her long skirt was caught in one of her wire sculptures, and she tugged frantically until it ripped free, but her path was blocked by heaps of burning rubble.

I gestured to Jerry. "The pond!"

Fortunately, Phoebe's collection of junk included pots, buckets, and the old washtub she'd asked Zack to lift down for her the other day. Jerry and Zack grabbed the washtub and scooped up water from the pond while Jake used a piece of rake to clear debris.

Phoebe ran out just as the roof gave way and fell in a crumbling mass of flaming timbers. We backed away, coughing and shielding our faces from the ashes. As sirens sounded in the distance, we retreated to the side of the road.

Zack held on to Phoebe. "Are you all right? What happened? You're always so careful around your stuff."

She clung to him, her face smudged, her pale hair in disarray. "I don't know! I was finishing my twist tie wreath when I thought I heard a car drive up. Before I could get to the front, I heard a car door slam and brakes squeal as it drove away. That's when I smelled smoke."

The mysterious speeding silver car? "Did you see the car?" I asked.

"No, I ran to the holiday aisle where I keep all my Christmas things. I thought maybe I'd left some candles burning. Then everything went up so fast! I couldn't believe it."

After seeing the piles of flammable materials Phoebe used for her art, I could believe it.

"Oh, gosh, there goes 'Baby Dear'!" Phoebe cried. "I really liked that one."

One after another, Phoebe's creations went up in flames. The fire trucks arrived in time to save most of her little cottage, but the barn studio was a total loss. We stood back out of the way while Jake recorded the activity around him, and Zack and Phoebe talked with the fire chief and EMTs.

After a while, Zack came up to me, his expression determined.

"Madeline, I've decided to come clean with Phoebe about my affair with her mother. If she hates me, then I'll have to deal with it, but this fire—" He stopped, took a breath, and continued. "This fire has scared the hell out of me. I think Roxanna had something to do with this. She's trying to keep me in line, but I've had enough of it."

"What does she have over you, Zack, besides the affair?" I asked. "If you tell Phoebe about the affair, Roxanna won't have any more power over you."

"There's another thing."

There was more? Wagner could've written this case. "What's that?"

"She'll tell *my* mother, and the world will implode."

Yup, positively Wagnarian. "Why would Letticia care, other than you're seeing a woman her age?"

"They used to be friends back when they were both struggling artists. My mother had early success and Roxanna resented this. She also thought that Letticia should have used her influence to help her career, but instead she trashed it. Roxanna plays nice on the museum board, but that's all for show. She's incredibly jealous."

I knew all that, but there was one thing I couldn't figure out. "Okay, let me get this straight. You knew Roxanna hated your mother, yet you slept with her?"

He hung his head, his face flushed with shame. "I'm not proud of that. I was angry because I didn't get an exhibit in the museum. I thought I could get back at my mother by sleeping with the enemy. Well, I got more than I bargained for."

"What do you know about the missing paintings?" I asked.

"I swear I don't know anything," he said. "But I didn't tell you the whole truth. Phoebe and I snuck into the museum last Tuesday night."

"I thought you said your mother had that back door lock changed."

"Yeah, well, I might have lied about that."

"Why did you break in?"

"I wanted to see the paintings in the gala, but there was someone in there, someone taking the paintings off the walls. We got out of there as fast as we could."

"You didn't see who it was?"

"No, I didn't want to get involved."

"You didn't think to call the police?"

"And have to explain why Phoebe and I were there? Might have just been someone rearranging things."

I was certainly tired of talking to Zack. "Maybe Phoebe knew who it was."

Jerry came up to us with Phoebe. "She's okay. The EMTs said she didn't need to go to the hospital."

Zack ran to her and hugged her. "Thank God you're all right. Let's go back to my place so you can rest. Then we need to talk."

"No," she said. "I need to talk to Madeline. Is there someplace we can sit down and talk privately?"

"Sure," he said. He led us back to his studio and motioned to a circle of wide stones in the back yard. "You can sit out here."

With a couple of anxious glances at Phoebe, Zack walked away. Phoebe sat down and pulled the remains of her tattered skirt around her. I sat across from her.

"Let's hear it."

"I'm ready," she said. "I've been ready for a long time. I've just been too afraid to say anything. I don't know what your relationship is like with your mother."

"Prickly," I said.

She gave a wan smile. "Maybe you'll understand, then. I've never been able to please my mother. I know she thinks I'm useless, but I don't have her ambition, her insane need to be perfect. She's never supported me, so I have no idea why I feel I should protect her. But Tuesday night Zack took me into the museum, and we saw someone taking the paintings down off the walls. I knew that was my mother. I wanted to believe she was only fixing the exhibit, but the next day, when we found out the paintings were missing, I knew she'd taken them."

She took a deep sigh and looked around at the chunks of stone scattered across the yard. The stones resembled pieces of a giant jig-saw puzzle, like the puzzle Phoebe was struggling to solve.

"So I went to see her at her home the next day. I—I wanted to be wrong. Or if she did steal the paintings, I wanted to know why, or help her find a way out, or something. She was not happy to see me, but then, she never is. We went into her study. I asked her why she was in the museum last night. I thought she was going to leap over her desk and attack me. 'How the hell did you know that?' she said. I told her Zack and I snuck in. Then she slammed her fist down and said, 'That idiot!'"

My mother was getting kinder and sweeter by the minute.

Phoebe looked past the stones to where Zack stood watching us forlornly from a safe distance. "I don't know why she was so angry with him."

I did, but I kept that to myself. "Did you ask her if she took the paintings?"

"Yes. She said no, that was ridiculous and how dare I accuse her of such a thing. There was a stack of paintings in the corner, all turned toward the wall. I asked her about them. She said that was none of my business, but if I had to know, they were paintings she was going to use in a display about the museum in the Thirties."

Was it possible the stolen paintings were in Roxanna's house? Did I finally have a chance of recovering *Blue Moon Garden*? "These paintings you saw. Can you tell me anything else about them? The sizes, the frames? Were they damaged in any way?"

"Like I said, they were turned toward the wall, so I couldn't see what they were. They were different sizes and had different frames. They looked okay, I guess. Oh, one frame was silver. I remember that."

Blue Moon Garden had a silver frame.

Phoebe's eyes filled with tears. "I'm sorry I caused so much trouble, Madeline. I only wanted her approval. I see now that's impossible."

"What about the fire?" I asked. "Would she go so far as to destroy your studio?"

"I don't know," she said. "I'm beginning to believe she's capable of anything."

She put her face down in her hands and sobbed. I motioned for Zack to come over. "You and Phoebe need to talk."

He nodded and took my place next to her.

Jerry had waited by my car. Jake circled back to us. "I've got enough material here for a blockbuster episode, Madeline. What did Phoebe have to say?"

No need to broadcast Phoebe's heartache or Zack's involvement with her mother until he'd had a chance to come clean with Letticia. I also needed to confront Roxanna. If she knew where *Blue Moon Garden* was, she'd better tell me. "You want a big story, you might want to wait until I've got all the facts."

His grin widened. "Yes, ma'am. How 'bout I take the footage I've got today and edit it for you to approve later?"

"That would be excellent, thank you."

He gave me a little salute and trotted off to the Gremlin.

"Well, we had a fiery mountain," Jerry said. "A fiery mountain of trash. But still, a mountain on fire."

"Only this Brunnhilda wasn't asleep, thank goodness."

"I can't make Brunnhilda out of Phoebe, no matter how I try."

I filled Jerry in on all the details of my conversation with Phoebe. "I'm almost certain that was Roxanna's car that tried to run us over. She set fire to Phoebe's studio as a warning to her not to say anything about the paintings."

Jerry agreed that Roxanna was the clear winner for Evil Mother of the Year. "And a warning to Zack to keep quiet, too."

"I need to find a way to search her house," I said.

"You know I can get us in."

"Let me try the direct approach," I said. "I'll simply ask her."

CHAPTER SIXTEEN

Roxanna was not in her office. A helpful docent said she'd gone out to have lunch with some of the other board members.

"Gone out to have lunch or to set fire to Phoebe's studio?" I said to Jerry.

While we were there, we had a look in Roxanna's office. There were no paintings except her own stark black and white pen and ink drawings hanging on the walls. It was too much to hope the paintings were stacked behind her desk or stuffed in her closet, although I looked to make sure. "Roxanna's house is looking more and more promising," I said.

"We can head over there right now."

But before we could set off, Jerry's phone rang. He answered, listened a moment, and then said "She's what? Are you sure? Did you try Pot Luck Alley? Damn. No, don't call them yet. I'm on it, thanks." He ended the call. "That was Rusty. Susie's missing."

"Missing?" I said.

"She was supposed to check in this morning and never showed, never sent a password, nothing. Rusty wanted to enlist Helen's Angels to search for her, but I told him to wait."

I had no idea what was going on. "Check in? Check in with who? What could have happened?"

"Well, I'm hoping she had to go underground for a few days. There's one way I can find out. Come on."

***

I'd been to the pawn shop in Pot Luck Alley. I'd been to a few other sketchy places Jerry used to frequent. But I hadn't been to Quarter Street on the corner of Dime Avenue just off Dollar Boulevard.

"What, no Penny Lane?" I asked as we made our way down the quiet little tree-lined street.

"There's a safe house down here," Jerry said.

"I hate to sound paranoid, but are you sure this isn't a trap?"

"I'll know in a minute."

He pulled up in front of a modest home covered in ivy. There were flower pots filled with pink and purple petunias on a garden bench. A wheelbarrow sat on one side of the bench, overflowing with grass cuttings.

"All clear," Jerry said.

"And you know this because—?"

"Because the wheelbarrow is right side up."

We got out of the car and went up the curved flagstone walkway. Under the arch of the porch was a bright red door with a cheerful "Welcome" sign decorated with bluebirds.

"Is there a secret knock?" I asked.

"Just wait."

The door opened into a small foyer. Jerry led the way into a parlor with a sofa and chairs that reminded me of the furniture in the Eberlin House before we remodeled, dark and Victorian with flowered upholstery and curved legs. On the back wall of this room was what appeared at first glance to be a door set in the center of an elaborate bookcase filled with leather bound books, silver candlesticks, small expensive looking glass vases, and bronze figures. The door was a rich mahogany color with an oval stained glass window and delicate scroll work along the sides.

Closer inspection revealed that the door and the bookcase were part of an expertly painted mural.

"Watch this," Jerry said. He pushed on the painted door, which swung open, revealing a hallway. The mural effectively hid the real way into the safe house. "Almost *tromp l'oeil*, isn't it?"

We stepped into a hallway to be greeted by Susie. "Hi, Jerry, Madeline. Sorry for all the secrecy. Someone in the group was getting suspicious and I had to lie low."

Jerry gave her a hug. "I'm just glad you're okay. Look, if things are getting too hot, maybe you oughta bow out."

"Not now," she said. "They are stepping up their plan."

"Can I ask what plan?" I said.

"Come have a seat," she said.

She led us into a living room that wouldn't have looked out of place in a *Good Housekeeping Magazine*, circa 1950. The long sofa and matching chair with flared legs were in a shade of gold, as well as the gold drum shades on the end table lamp and hanging lamp. In the corner sat a combination turn table, TV, and radio bookshelf. It was the size of a small chest freezer.

"Is this someone's actual home?" I asked.

"We own it under the name of Agnes Groody," she said. "She's eighty-five and reclusive and known to threaten strangers and neighbors with a shotgun. Nobody bothers her."

"Let me guess," I said. "You are Agnes."

She smiled her first smile of the visit. "And you are right."

She sat down in the chair, and Jerry and I took the sofa. "Tell me what's going on," he said.

She leaned forward. "I was supposed to check in with Rusty this morning, but I thought I'd better hold off because things are heating up. Here's what I know so far. You've got Caldwell in charge. Do you know him?"

"I know who he is, but I never worked with him. He was before my time."

"He's calling the shots. But he's also called in a couple of heavies to do the dirty work."

"Whoa, hold on here," I said. "'Dirty work'? They're not planning to attack Jerry, are they?"

"Caldwell will give him a chance to switch sides."

Which he would never do. "Well, that's comforting."

"It won't come to that," Jerry said. "Do they know where I live, Susie?"

"I'm afraid so."

Oh, I did not like this, at all. "When you say 'heavies,' what do you mean?" I asked.

"Another thing I'm trying to find out," Susie said. "I think Caldwell hired them from Thugs R Us. I'll keep you posted through Rusty, I promise."

"Rusty and the Angels can take on anyone," he said.

She reached over and patted his arm. "There you go. I feel better already."

***

I did not feel better and told Jerry so all the way home.

"Mac, there are plenty of people on Big Mike's side who can prevent any sort of thuggery," he said. "Besides, Big Mike is keeping an eye on all this via Susie and other spies. If Caldwell makes a move, it'll all be over for him."

He was taking a much too light-hearted approach to this threat. "Just don't go anywhere by yourself for a while," I said. I took out my phone. "Now let's see what Roxanna has to say about a visit."

"Well, this is most inconvenient," she said when I asked if Jerry and I could stop by. "I'm getting ready to return to the museum, but I suppose I could spare a few minutes. Is there any particular reason we need to meet here?"

"Phoebe saw you in the museum late Tuesday night, taking the gala paintings off the walls. She saw paintings in your house the next day."

"For my display. I told her that." Roxanna's voice was calm. Then she gave an odd little laugh. "Perhaps you should come over, after all."

"Okay, that was weird," I told Jerry. "She seemed to find the situation amusing."

We drove to Roxanna's house, located in an older Parkland neighborhood called Longwood. All the houses were small brick homes. Roxanna's silver Accord was parked out front. I'd hoped to find it covered in dust, but even more interesting, it was sparkling clean.

"Think she drove it through the car wash on her way home?"

I asked Jerry.

"That's what I would do."

We walked up onto the tiny front porch. I rang the door bell.

Roxanna opened the door. She welcomed us in pleasantly enough, but her dark gaze was hard and calculating. Her house, like my mother's, was a study in black and white, but unlike Mom's, the furnishings were minimal and the atmosphere chilly. She invited us into the living room where Jerry and I sat on spindly little black chairs and Roxanna arranged herself in a white arm chair.

"Now, tell me again why you think the gala paintings are here? I told Phoebe the paintings she saw here were part of my 'A Walk Back in Time' display."

"She saw you take the gala paintings off the wall. What did you do with them?"

"I have no idea what you're talking about."

"Phoebe told me one of the paintings she saw here had a silver frame," I said. "I've seen the paintings you chose for your display. I don't recall any one of them having a silver frame. But my painting does. Where is *Blue Moon Garden*?"

A slow smile curved her mouth. "You think I stole them, don't you?" She leaned forward. "Well, how about this? You and your husband may search every inch of my home. Take your time. I defy you to find anything. In fact, if you want to call the police and have them help you search, you go right ahead."

"They must not be here, or you wouldn't agree to a search," I said.

"Aren't you clever? Clever enough to find the paintings? I don't think so."

Jerry gave me a nod and left the living room. Roxanna leaned back in her chair, and smirked. She had thrown down her challenge.

"You know where they are," I said.

She shrugged. "You're the great detective. You figure it out."

"I can call the police."

"And say what? Without proof, it's your word against mine, and I don't think the Parkland Police Department gives a damn about some dinky little investigator from Celosia, a former beauty queen, no less." She waved a hand. "So go ahead and search all you like."

I felt an almost overwhelming urge to smack her self-satisfied face, but I kept my temper and went to find Jerry. He was in the kitchen, looking through the cabinets.

"I've already checked the stove and the fridge," he said. "We'll play along for now, but there's bound to be a clue."

"She's dared me to find them," I said. "If I go to Jordan Finley without proof, he'll laugh me out of town."

"Then we'll find proof."

We stubbornly stayed and looked through every room, but we didn't find anything in Roxanna's house.

She saw us out. "I hope this is the last I'll see of you two," she said. "Otherwise I'll call the police myself. I don't like being harassed."

She slammed the door. I would have liked to have screamed a primal scream, but I settled for a frustrated sigh. "Round one to Roxanna, damn it."

"True," Jerry said, "but there's always round two."

CHAPTER SEVENTEEN

On the way home, I thought of all the things that had happened at the museum and how Roxanna could have orchestrated them all.

"She had motive and opportunity," I told Jerry. "She has a key and knows the security codes, so she can get into the museum any time she likes. She could've taken the grant proposal off Letticia's desk. She probably knew the Halsey painting was a fake. She could've called Specialty Transport and cancelled the playground equipment order. The secretary I spoke with said a woman called in the cancellation."

"All because Letticia gave her a bad review? That's not much of a motive."

"But Letticia has always gotten everything Roxanna wanted, the art school scholarship, the museum job, an editor position with *Artistic Review*. And did you see her tiny house and her economy car? She's jealous as hell. Having an affair with Letticia's son isn't enough for her. Stealing the paintings and hiding them away was her grand finale. I'll bet if I don't find them, she'll 'find' them and save the museum."

"How would she explain that?" Jerry asked.

"I don't know," I said, "but I'm not going to give her that opportunity."

***

At home, Hayden and Denisha had set up their production company on the porch and were surrounded by stacks of colored paper and ribbons. Denisha held up a booklet with a glittery cover. "Here's my poetry book!"

"Wow, that is beautiful," I said.

She handed it to me and gave Jerry one. "We're making copies for everybody, and then we'll make more for my book signing."

Jerry sat on the porch rail and admired each page. "These are excellent poems, Denisha."

"Hayden says I have real talent and that I'm very good at self-editing."

Hayden brushed glitter off his hands. "She's a good critic, too."

"Oh, yes, I read his poems and told him when I couldn't understand things. There's no reason to write poems no one can understand. He's getting better at it."

I caught Hayden's eye, and he grinned. "Lesson learned."

"Read them the one about your mother, Hayden. It's really good."

"Maybe later," he said.

Hayden and Denisha stacked the poetry books and cleaned up the leftover paper and ribbon. Denisha thanked Hayden and rode off on her bike.

He watched her ride down the bumpy trail through the fields. "I should be thanking her. Repeatedly. I think she saved my career."

"By telling you to stop being obscure?"

"By reminding me that writing is fun. I was to the point that it was a chore, almost torture. I'd forgotten how much joy it brings me." He gestured to the front yard. "And this setting couldn't be better. These beautiful peaceful fields, the flowers, the woods off in the distance."

"You are welcome on our porch anytime," I said. "Did you find out anything from Roxanna?"

"The meeting went as you hoped," he said. "There weren't enough board members present for a deciding vote. Roxanna sounded disappointed."

"I'll bet she did. That's the only thing not going her way."

"What do you mean?" Hayden asked.

"Someone set fire to Phoebe's studio. She's okay, but the barn's a total loss."

"Set fire to—?" His voice quit for a minute. "You don't think Roxanna's responsible?"

"Yes," I said. "We passed a silver car speeding away from her studio a few minutes before the studio caught fire. Roxanna drives a silver Accord." I explained that Phoebe saw her mother take the paintings and how Roxanna had dared me to find them.

Hayden was amazed. "So, Roxanna stole the paintings? Why not go to the police?"

"Because right now, unless I find them, it's her word against mine."

"I hate to say this, Madeline, but what if she sold them, or worse, destroyed them?"

I'd thought of this, too. "If she sells them, we'll definitely find them, because descriptions and pictures have been all over the place on the news and in the *Herald.* As for destroying them—well, Roxanna's having a great time showing me and Letticia how much smarter she is. I don't think she'll destroy the paintings. She might 'find' them and take all the credit."

"Sounds pretty brazen."

"That's an excellent word for her. I've encountered a lot of criminals and murderers, but this is the first time one has challenged me to catch her."

"All of the killers Mac's caught have been women," Jerry pointed out.

"Is that true?" Hayden asked me.

"You're right. My first case involved a washed up pageant queen, the second was a lovelorn librarian, the third was an illegitimate daughter who thought she was entitled to an inheritance, the fourth was a frustrated artist, and the two murderers from my last case were both women. Must be all this fresh country air that sets them off."

"'Lovelorn librarian,'" Hayden said. "I like that. But I don't like the idea of anyone's house being deliberately set on fire."

"Me, either," I said. "Just because this case isn't a murder case now doesn't mean someone might get hurt or killed." This made me think of my own house sitting out here a mile from town in the middle of a field. Would those thugs Susie mentioned attempt something like setting fire to our home? Jerry said he never worked with Caldwell, so how would Caldwell know him, unless someone else decided to expose him. The convolutions of all this inter-gang war were driving me crazy. I wished Big Mike would just show up and mow them all down.

For dinner, Jerry made homemade pizzas on grilled flat bread with a variety of toppings gleaned from the fridge. This met with my approval because by now, I was starving and would've eaten the fridge if I could've gotten it between two slices of bread.

"I want to talk to Big Mike," I said. "I want him to take care of this other problem we're having."

Jerry's eyebrows rose. "You want to owe him another favor?"

I paused to rescue a hunk of tomato that was going over the side of my fourth piece of pizza. "Well, he's practically family now, isn't he? He might do it for nothing."

"He doesn't do anything for nothing. Call your mom. I bet she knows where he is right now."

It had been another day oddly devoid of my mother's anxious phone calls. I had to admit I was curious to know what was going on. After four rings, her answering machine clicked on, and I left a message. "Hi, just calling to see how you're doing. Love you."

I set my phone down on the table. "I guess she and Big Mike have sailed off to Hawaii on his yacht."

Hayden reached for another slice. "Are they that serious?"

"I don't know what's happening."

"But it's okay, isn't it? Your mother's been upset over the break-in."

I didn't know why I was letting this bother me. "I guess I'm not used to having a happy mom. Even when I won a Little Miss pageant, she was never satisfied."

He put another scoop of cheese on his pizza. "Mine was always afraid something would happen to me. Nothing ever did, of course, but that didn't keep her from worrying."

Jerry refilled our tea glasses. "Do I need to make more food?"

Hayden indicated the slice of pizza on his plate. "This'll do it for me."

"Mac?"

I had eaten plenty of pizza, but there was still a little room. "What's for dessert?"

***

While we were enjoying huge slices of peach pie with ice cream, Jerry's accompanist replacement Sandy called, asking for help with a tricky part of the *Flower of the South* score and could Jerry stop by the rehearsal. Since I didn't want Jerry going anywhere alone, and I needed a distraction from my rough day, Hayden and I decided to tag along. We sat in the back of the auditorium while Jerry went down to the orchestra pit.

The director clapped his hands and called for attention. "Okay, folks, we have two and a half weeks before opening night. I know that sounds like a lot of time, but it really isn't. We need to tighten up the acts and keep the pace going, or our audiences will think they're watching a documentary on how grapes grow. So places for act one, and keep it moving."

Unlike the Rossboro show, in which Emmaline aged from young woman to the older version played by Joanie, in the Celosia production Emmaline was played by one of Deely's waitresses, Annie Vernon, a young woman who stayed young throughout the entire show. According to people who know these things, North Carolina had once been a land of vineyards before Sir Walter Raleigh was introduced to tobacco. Wine and cigarettes. What a legacy.

Annie came center stage. The orchestra played an introduction, and she launched into song.

"Oh, here is where I long to be,
The mountains blue as the restless sea.
Here is where I plant my vines,
Here I create my fragrant wines!"

There were several other verses, my favorite being, "Here is where I truly belong as I grow my scuppernong." I always thought "scuppernong" was a funny word for a type of grape, and Jerry couldn't wait to work it into a song.

As act one unfolded with its scenes of hardy settlers landing in North Carolina and finding land for their vineyards, Hayden leaned forward in his seat. "So far, so good. I'm riveted."

"It gets better."

Emmaline's parents were suitably appalled at the idea of their daughter having her own vineyard and tried to discourage her. Emmaline struck a brave pose and sang her I Know I'm Only A Girl, But I Can Do This song, "I'm Emmaline." The other settlers responded with skepticism and downright mean faces, but Emmaline sang on, undaunted. Soon her parents relented and gave her a tiny piece of land. The settlers sang a version of It'll Never Work, the parents sang a couple of verses of Do You Know What You're Doing? Emmaline closed act one with a fervent show stopping number along the lines of One Day You'll See And You Will All Bow Before Me. At least, those are the titles Hayden and I made up to entertain ourselves.

The director was pleased with the time and called for a ten minute break before they moved on to act two, which opened with a terrible storm that ruined Emmaline's first crop and set her into depression and another song. But she rallied, started over, and soon, after an interpretive dance that recreated the growth of grapes on the vine, had the best-looking if freakishly large grapes anyone had ever seen.

"Jerry wanted a kick line of grapes that sang louder as they ripened, but this didn't suit the director's vision," I told Hayden.

"Too bad. I would've liked to have seen that."

Emmaline's crop saved the town, the settlers realized they had been judgmental and wrong, and the show ended with a harvest festival, singing, dancing, and generous amounts of wine.

"Tourists are going to love it," Hayden said. "It's historically accurate, too. I remember my great-grandpa telling me about the basketball sized grapes he used to eat. One squeeze and you had a party."

"I don't see how Rossboro can compete with this."

The director gave some notes, including a reminder to the cast not to wear their historically inaccurate wristwatches and nose rings. Jerry then came up the aisle.

"What did you think?"

"It was everything I imagined and more," I said.

"Very entertaining and educational," Hayden said. "The rhyming of 'spoilt' and 'boilt' was especially dramatic."

"I knew you'd like that. Mac, I think I'll write a sequel. How about *The Twisted Vine: Emmaline's Revenge*?"

"That's fine," I said. "And when Amanda hears about it, you can deal with her."

"And her rottenness."

As we left the auditorium, I realized I still hadn't heard from my mother. "I'd better give Mom another call. It's not like her to be off the radar this long."

Mom answered on the first ring. "Oh, Madeline, I was just getting ready to call you. I've had the best day."

I almost dropped my phone. "Well, that's good to hear."

"Michael and I went to the Biltmore House for lunch! Can you imagine? He was able to get a reservation, and we took his private limousine. I had a wonderful time."

The Biltmore House in Asheville was the closest thing to a castle in the state, an elegant two hundred and fifty room mansion that was the former home of George Vanderbilt and now open to the public. I turned to relay this information to Jerry and Hayden. "Big Mike took her to the Biltmore House for lunch." Back to Mom. "That sounds great. Where are you now? Is Michael still there?"

"No, he had some business to attend to, so he brought me home. Did you have some news for me about the crime?"

Roxanna Deluca is the thief, I wanted to say. She's responsible for everything that's happened at the museum, but I don't have any proof. "Still working on it, Mom."

"All right. Let me know. Good night."

She sounded so reasonable and calm, I couldn't believe it. "I will. Good night." I turned to Jerry. "Big Mike's already left, so I couldn't ask about another favor. The Biltmore House! Can you believe it?"

"That kept her mind off her troubles," Jerry said.

But my mind was saying, is Big Mike stepping up his game? Is he really serious about my mother? "I suppose I should be happy, but I'm not sure how to feel."

"If at any time your mom wants to call this off, she can. I say let her have some good times for a change."

"You're right. I should be glad."

But I couldn't shake those pesky uncomfortable feelings and thought about them late into the night when I should have been sleeping. What if she finds out what Big Mike really does for a living? What if she thinks Jerry and I played a trick on her? What if she falls in love with Big Mike? Jerry insisted Big Mike was honorable in his dealings with women, but did he know everything about his mentor? What if some of Big Mike's enemies decided to use my mother against him? What if she distracted Big Mike when he should be paying attention to the takeover plot?

There was so much potential for real danger here.

I gave my bedside clock a bleary glance. Okay, three o'clock in the morning is not the best time for reasonable thought. If I was going to obsess, I should be concentrating on my case. I should be worrying about *Blue Moon Garden*. I was so close! I couldn't let Roxanna Deluca win. There had to be a way to trick her into revealing my painting's hiding place.

I got up and went in search of food. This time, Hayden wasn't in the kitchen to surprise me. I had the place all to myself. I stood at the windows with the jar of peanut butter and a spoon. The stars looked close enough to touch, and at the edge of the woods, a few deer munched at the meadow grass. A whippoorwill's odd looping whistle echoed softly. I'd read somewhere that Native Americans believed the whippoorwill had the ability to capture lost souls and take them to their final resting place. Whether this was true or not didn't matter. Being carted from hotel to hotel as a child, I'd never heard a whippoorwill until I moved to Celosia, and I loved the sound. I could imagine a lost soul being charmed by the haunting song and following it through the dark.

Perhaps the song had led Hayden's mother to peace. And Jerry's parents.

For now, the song was peaceful enough that I could go back to bed and sleep.

CHAPTER EIGHTEEN

Tuesday morning, Hayden had his usual call from Shana to see how he was doing. He gave Jerry and me this information as we waited on Jerry's hash browns and eggs to finish frying. "I told her I was okay because I was helping you with a case."

I wish I could've seen Shana's face when she heard that. "What did she say?"

"She thought that was a great idea as long as I didn't get in the way."

"At this point, my case is so up in the air, you can't get in the way."

I checked my phone. No message from Mom.

Jerry scooped up a generous portion of hash browns and eggs and put them on a plate for me. "Maybe Big Mike slept over."

My mind wouldn't go there. "I still can't believe he took my mother all the way to Asheville for lunch yesterday."

"Better start practicing calling him Big Dad."

He and Hayden thought this was funny, and after attempting a withering look, I had to grin.

***

Despite Jerry's protests that he would be perfectly safe driving to work, I gave him a ride to Deely's and then drove on to the museum. I couldn't shake the feeling I was missing something. What had Roxanna done with the paintings?

The museum had just opened, and there were only a few visitors. The door to Letticia's office was closed. Roxanna's office was open, but she wasn't there, which gave me a chance to look around. But, as before, there was nothing to see.

I walked down to the Museum in the Thirties display, hoping to catch her there. No luck. I stood for a long time looking at the paintings. They were beautifully arranged. The railroad station scene, the boats, the workers at the printing press, plus seven more, all different sizes, but in the matching frames that tied the display together. The frames were exceptionally thick, especially along the sides. I wasn't up on my Frame Styles of the Thirties, but assumed they were authentic to the period.

I heard footsteps and turned to see Letticia walking up to me.

"It turned out well, didn't it?" she said.

"It's very well done," I said.

"It should be. Roxanna worked day and night to get it ready."

She looked tired. "How are you doing?" I asked. "I hear the board meeting didn't go as some people had planned."

"No, but they'll try again. Maybe by then, the paintings will be found, and I'll have a few more supporters than detractors."

"Did you hear about Phoebe's studio?"

"That was all Roxanna could talk about this morning. She said she wasn't surprised because of all the trash Phoebe kept in her barn. Thank goodness no one was hurt."

So no motherly concern there. And it didn't sound as if Zack had gathered up the courage to talk to his mother.

I took one last look at the display, wondering why I couldn't put my finger on what was bothering me about it, then left. I found Roxanna's silver Accord in the parking lot and looked it over once more for any possible sign the car had been at Phoebe's yesterday. There wasn't so much as a scratch on the sleek finish.

***

When I returned home, Hayden was on the porch with his notebook. I joined him there.

I felt discouraged and wasn't really in the mood for Jake when the purple Gremlin zipped up the drive and came to a halt under the trees. Jake popped out. He had on his yellow shirt and orange and red flame tie.

"Wait till you see this, Madeline! Hiya, Hayden. Have a look."

Jake positioned his phone so Hayden and I could see the video of Phoebe's studio engulfed in smoke and flames. There were a few jerky scenes where Jake put his phone down to help, and then more shots of Phoebe's creations twisting and spiraling up into sparks and ash. Jake had then recorded her safe in Zack's arms and the arrival of the fire trucks and ambulance. Occasionally the camera panned to me.

"Lookin' good and serious there," Jake commented.

"I hope so. I wouldn't want to be waving at the crowd at this point."

The video ended with one last view of the ruined studio. "Whadda you think? Add some voice over, some dramatic music."

Although the footage was intense, the violence wasn't gratuitous, and everyone was unharmed. "I think it's good," I said.

"Sure, sure. Anything going on today?"

The last thing I wanted was to get Jake involved in a Con World Take Over. "No, but the video's great, really."

Jake took a moment to perch on the porch rail like a hummingbird. "This could be shaping up to be a Big Story, you know."

"It could happen," I said.

"It *will* happen." He hopped up. "Okay, back to the *Galaxy* to see what Basil's got lined up for me now. Don't worry, Madeline. We're gonna blow this case wide open."

Off he went.

Blow this case wide open.

Jerry's old life was intruding on my peace in a major way, I had to find the missing paintings, and my mother was dating Big Mike.

There's your problem right there, I told myself. Three problems. Problems that are bugging you more than you realize.

Hayden's voice brought me back to the present. "Madeline, you have another visitor. It's your biggest fan."

Rusty had already parked and unwedged himself from his Corvette. He said a brief "Hello" to Hayden. He touched the brim of his hat. "Miss Parkland."

"Good morning," I said. "I'm glad you stopped by. Do you know anything more about this take over plot?"

"No," he said. "Thanks for checking on Susie. She's put herself in a tight spot."

"Can't she just leave?"

"She's in too far now. Don't worry. Things are under control."

I wished I could believe him.

He parked himself on the top step. "Wanted you to know things are progressing for the Miss Streetwise Pageant. Got the garage all decked out, got the band. I think we're good to go. You want to write a poem about it?"

This last question was addressed to Hayden, who looked taken aback. "Uh, sure, okay."

"My girlfriend read your book. Said it was hard going, but she liked it."

"Oh, um, thank you."

"If you write one for the pageant, it needs to make sense."

"I'll do that."

Rusty turned back to me. "I'll be in touch."

Hayden and I watched as he squeezed into the Corvette, and as soon as he was down the drive, we burst into laughter.

"I can't wait to tell Jerry," I said.

Hayden reached for his notebook. "I've never written a poem about a beauty pageant at a custom car shop. Now, there's a challenge."

***

It was time to pick Jerry up at Deely's.

He'd hopped in the passenger's seat and clicked on his seat belt when my phone rang. I looked at the caller ID. "Joanie Raines. Good grief. What now?"

"Let it go to voice mail," Jerry said.

"No, I'd better see what she wants. She may have murdered Amanda."

Joanie's shriek almost made me drop my phone. "Madeline! Amanda's new husband has bought our show!"

"Bought your show? What do you mean? How can he do that?"

"He offered the playwright a hundred thousand dollars for the rights to the drama! That means Stratton will own the show, and he can do whatever he wants with it, and you know what he'll do! He'll make it into the Amanda Show."

"Wait," I said. "Calm down. Are you sure this is true? Did the playwright accept the offer?"

"What idiot turns down a hundred thousand dollars?"

She hadn't mentioned what I considered the more important issue. "Speaking of money, what did the Arts Council say when you brought back the five thousand dollars?"

"Oh," she said, her tone subdued. "They were pretty understanding, They all know how Amanda is. They're not going to press charges, but they said because of the circumstances, I'd have to leave the show."

"I'm sorry. I know the show means a lot to you."

"No, it's all my fault. I let my hatred get in the way of common sense. I can still help out, though. Hand out programs, things like that." Once again, her voice was on the rise. "But that's not important! I'm at Pete's Bar and Grill right now, right across from the Arts Council. We're all here trying to figure out how we can stop Amanda from buying our show!"

"Hold on a moment." I turned to Jerry, who was waiting with an amused expression. "Joanie and the Arts Council members are at Pete's Bar and Grill having a meltdown over Anderson Stratton's possible hostile takeover of Rossboro's Emmaline play. How important is this?"

"Can Joanie get the facts?"

"Joanie," I said. "Call me when you are absolutely sure this is true." I ended the call on her spluttering reply.

Then Jerry's phone rang with a call from the director at Celosia's community theater. I heard only one side of the conversation, enough to know Amanda was attacking on all fronts.

"He is?" Jerry said. "Is this a serious offer? Yeah, Mac just had a similar call from Joanie. Okay, no problem. Sure, be right there."

He ended the call. "Stratton wants to buy *Flower of the South*, too, and since the music belongs to me, I'd better see what's going on. Why don't we stop by the theater?"

***

I had turned down Main Street towards the Baker Auditorium, home of Celosia's community theater, when Jerry's phone rang again. This time I could hear the caller. It was Susie, and she was sobbing for real.

He put his phone on speaker so I could hear. "What's wrong?" he asked her.

"Where are you?" she said, her voice frantic. "You're not at your house, are you? Caldwell wanted to know where you were. He was going to kill me if I didn't tell them. I—I had to, Jerry. You have to get out. He's sent those two men after you."

"Calm down," he said. "I'm not there. Where are you?"

She caught her breath on another sob. "I got away. I can't talk anymore." She ended the call.

What was going on? If Caldwell's henchmen went to the house to snatch Jerry, and he wasn't there—oh, no. No, no, no.

"Jerry, Hayden's at the house. Oh, my God, what if Austin and Denisha are there, too?"

CHAPTER NINETEEN

We broke every possible speed limit getting home. About the time we got there, Austin's four-wheeler bounced across the field. Austin skidded to a stop and jumped off.

"Madeline! Jerry! Two big guys came by and grabbed Hayden! I followed them as far as I could. They took him to the zombie house!"

"What about Denisha?" I asked. "Was she here?"

"She's at her cousin's."

Jerry jumped on the four-wheeler. "Give me your helmet." Austin handed it over. "Hop on, Mac. Austin, you stay here."

"Okay," he said, eyes wide. "Should I call nine-one-one?"

"Yes. We'll go get Hayden."

He gulped. "Take the shortcut through the woods."

I got on behind Jerry and strapped on the spare helmet. I hung on as Jerry revved the engine and took off. We careened across the fields and down the narrow pathway through the trees, bumping over roots and rocks. At one point, I feared the uneven terrain would be too much for the four-wheeler, but the Polaris 570 was up to the task, and Jerry countered each dip and turn like a pro. We slid down a slight incline and barreled through another section of the woods, scattering pine cones and branches.

I had no idea what we would find at Austin's haunted house. For Hayden's safety, the last thing I wanted was a fire fight between Caldwell's men and the police, but some kind of back up would be useful. I thought first of Big Mike, but the one time I needed him I used a number he said was good for only one call. Maybe he was with Mom. Clinging to Jerry with one hand, I punched in her number.

She answered on the second ring. "Goodness, Madeline, what is that roaring sound?"

"Austin's four-wheeler. Mom, is Michael with you? I need to talk to him right now."

"No, but he's coming by later. I can hardly hear you. Tell Austin to drive somewhere else."

We hit a tree root and I almost lost my grip. "Oof! Do you have his number?"

"Madeline, what's going on?"

"Do you have Michael's phone number?"

"No, but I'll have him call you when he gets here. He's such a nice man. So considerate. We're going to the opera this weekend. Isn't Jerry a fan of the opera? Maybe the two of you could come with us. Oh, and Michael has some wonderful ideas to help the museum."

A tree branch smacked my shoulder. Another branch almost smacked the phone from my hand. "Mom, I've got to go. Call you later. Big Mike's not there," I shouted in Jerry's ear. But there was another big guy I could call. I punched in Rusty's number and was glad to hear his gruff voice.

"What's up, Miss Parkland?"

"I need your help. Caldwell's men have kidnapped Hayden. They've taken him to an abandoned house near Bylow's Farm."

Jerry spoke over his shoulder. "It's half a mile from our house, but he can get to it on Old Pathway Road. There's a trail. He'll need a motorcycle or something with four-wheel drive."

I relayed this information to Rusty, all the while hanging on, ducking low tree branches.

"Be right there," he said.

I put my phone away as Jerry slowed. He turned the four-wheeler around and turned off the engine. "We'd better go the rest of the way on foot."

The woods leaned in, tangles of vines and ivy choking the tree trunks. Birds chirped and something skittered in the undergrowth. Startled by our presence, squirrels leaped in the branches. Jerry led the way down a faint trail. He motioned for silence and pointed. Up ahead, I caught a glimpse of a dark blue truck parked beside an old house.

This was my first visit to the zombie house. It was bigger than I imagined, an old gray farm house with broken windows and a sagging roof. Bricks from the crumbling chimney lay scattered on the ground. We didn't see anyone. I hated to think of Hayden in that place and hoped with all my heart he wasn't seriously injured or worse.

A man came out of the house, a very large man, his bald head gleaming in the sun. His foot went through the porch. He pulled free, cursing, shook his foot, and called out, "What does he want us to do now?"

The second man, also pro wrestler-sized, came around the side of the house. "Said to hold off until we hear from him."

I gripped Jerry's arm. "Jerry, what can we do?"

I don't know if Jerry had a plan, but as it turned out, we didn't need one. We heard the roar of not one motorcycle, but several. Rusty, in a black four by four pickup and Helen's Angels, burst out of the woods and surrounded the men in a blur of dust, leaves, and leather. There weren't any battle cries of "Hoyotoho," but there was plenty of fierce screaming that would have made the Valkyries proud.

Rusty, shotgun in hand, jumped out of the truck and began firing, pinning one man down behind the house. Helga and Orla tackled the other man to the ground with Sissy and Leeta joining in a moment later in a tangle of gouging fingernails. The man yelped and unsuccessfully tried to shake them off.

Wallie followed Jerry and me as we made our cautious way through the shell of the old house, stepping carefully over gaping holes in the floorboards and easing around shaky support beams. Cobwebs shivered in broken windows, and a precariously leaning staircase led to the second floor. In the main room, Hayden lay sprawled by a fireplace. When I touched his shoulder, he groaned and opened his eyes.

"Madeline?"

"Yes, it's me. Are you okay?"

He winced. "I think my arm's broken."

"Can you get up?" He nodded. "Okay, we'll take it easy."

I helped him sit up. He held his left arm and looked around. He blinked a few times. "Oh, no. Is this the zombie house?"

I'd hoped we could get away before he realized this. "No zombies, just a couple of bad guys who're facing the wrath of Rusty and Helen's Angels." Outside, I could hear angry yells, battle cries, and the occasional gunshot that made me wince.

"Come on, buddy," Jerry said. "We need to get out of here." He and I got Hayden to his feet. Jerry slung Hayden's uninjured arm over his shoulder. "Watch where you step. This house is full of holes."

"I'll scout ahead," Wallie said.

"Madeline!" Rusty shouted. "Get out now!"

We made our cautious way to the front door. Wallie jumped off the porch to join the fight, and Rusty reached up and took Hayden. I sidestepped another beam as it teetered and fell, raising a cloud of dust. Coughing and waving the dust away, Jerry reached back to give me a hand and pulled me to safety.

I looked around. I could no longer refer to Helen's Angels as angels. There was nothing angelic about the way they dragged the unconscious henchmen to the edge of the woods and sat on them. It was pure Valkyrie. Rusty took a length of rope from the back of his truck and tossed it to the women. They used the rope to quickly hog-tie their prisoners. No chance of these men getting into Valhalla. They were destined for the Norse myth equivalent of prison.

Rusty motioned to Hayden, who was sitting by a tree. "I sat Hayden down over there out of the way." He jerked a thumb at the men. "How come they snatched Hayden?"

"They thought he was Jerry," I said.

He swung his gaze to Hayden and back to Jerry. "Yeah, I can see where they'd make that mistake. What do you want me to do with them?"

What did I want? I could hear sirens in the distance. "I need to explain things to Chief Brenner."

"All right. I'll be back up. Ladies?"

"We'll stay," Helga said. She poked the nearest man with her boot. "Just in case these two try anything else."

We heard the sirens stop, and in a few minutes, Chief of Police Gus Brenner and three armed police officers carefully approached through the woods.

"All clear," I called.

Chief Brenner's small sharp blue eyes took in the scene and motioned his officers forward. "All right," he said. "Let's hear it. Austin Terrell called nine-one-one and said, and I quote, 'Two men grabbed Hayden and carried him off to the zombie house.'"

"Yes, he's here," I said. "He has a broken arm, but otherwise, he's okay. Those two men over there are the kidnappers, but thanks to Rusty and Helen's Angels, we stopped them."

"We've got an ambulance on the way," Chief Brenner said.

"Hey," one of the men said. "We were just checking out this old house when these crazy women attacked us."

"You have the right to remain silent," Chief Brenner said, "and I suggest you do so." He gestured to an officer. "Read these men their rights and get them out of here." He spoke to Helga. "I'll need everyone's name and statement if you'll go with Officer Riggs." He turned to Rusty. "And you, sir?"

Rusty offered his huge hand. "Rusty Grant, co-owner of Streetwise Designs in Parkland. Madeline's helping me and the Angels with a pageant for the shop's anniversary. I'm a big fan of Miss Parkland here, so you better believe I came when she called."

Chief Brenner fixed me with his sharp gaze. "Why did these men kidnap Hayden?"

"They're from Jerry's past," I said. "They thought Hayden was Jerry."

Chief Brenner was familiar with Jerry's past. "I see. What did you do to annoy them, Jerry?"

"All I know is they were hired by a man named Caldwell," Jerry said. "That's all I can tell you."

Another siren wailed in the distance.

"That'll be the ambulance," the Chief said and dispatched another officer to lead the EMTs to the house. "Hayden, can you tell me what happened?"

"I was sitting on Madeline's porch, and those guys drove up, said, 'You're coming with us,' grabbed me by the arm, and that's the last thing I remember."

"All right. I'll have more questions later. Once we get this sorted out, you may want to press charges against these men."

As soon as Hayden was safely away in the ambulance and the Chief had finished with all of us, Jerry took the four-wheeler back to our house to check on Austin, while I rode with Rusty to the hospital.

***

Jerry met us in the hospital waiting area.

"Austin was full of questions," he said. "I thanked him for the loan of the four-wheeler and said we'd give him the full story later. He wanted to see the zombie house, but I convinced him Chief Brenner did not want him contaminating a crime scene, so he went home. How's Hayden?"

"He's almost ready to go. I think he was pleased to have an adventure."

"That's because he doesn't know how close he came to being killed."

"Yeah, we'd better leave out that part."

Rusty still had on his sunglasses and turned to give Jerry a blank stare. "What about Susie?"

"Mac wants us to leave that to Big Mike," he said. "I hope she made it back to the safe house. Aside from Caldwell, how many others are involved?"

"Nine or ten, I'd say. It's up to you."

Jerry didn't get a chance to answer because a nurse came down the hall pushing Hayden in a wheelchair. His left arm was in a cast and a sling, but he looked fine.

"Here you go, Mr. Amry," she said. "I believe these folks have come for you."

"I'll talk to you later," Jerry said to Rusty.

***

Jerry and I got Hayden settled in the guest room and had just come out to the porch when Austin and Denisha rode up on the four-wheeler. They jumped off, and we could hear Austin explaining everything.

"Then these big guys came right up on the porch and before Hayden could say anything, one said, 'You're coming with us, pal,' and the other one grabbed him by the arm. It was like something out of a movie only scarier because I could tell Hayden was hurt, and I didn't know what those guys were going to do. So I stayed back in the trees and then I followed them."

"It's lucky you were here," Denisha said.

"I'll say! Oh, hi, guys! I was just telling Denisha what she missed."

Jerry clapped him on the back. "Here's the real hero."

Austin looked surprised. "Who, me? I didn't do anything."

"Are you kidding? If you hadn't seen those men kidnap Hayden, we'd never have found him in time. Plus you let me and Mac use your four-wheeler to get to the zombie house."

"Oh, yeah, I guess I did."

"Is Hayden okay?" Denisha asked.

"Yes, he is. You can go up and see him if you like."

Hayden was awake and sitting up.

Austin was delighted. "You got a broken arm fighting off zombies! That's so cool."

Denisha sat down on the edge of the bed. "It's not the arm you write with, is it?"

"No, thank goodness. We can get back to our poetry pretty soon."

She gave a little bounce. "You'll have lots of new things to write about!"

Austin snorted. "Forget poetry! I wanna hear about the zombies."

"Me, too," Jerry said. "I'll get some snacks."

The kids heard several versions of the rescue and inhaled several bags of potato chips and cookies. When Hayden began to drift off, we all went downstairs.

Austin hurried to his four-wheeler. "My mom said if I'm not home by dark, she'll ground me. There's no way I'm telling her about the zombie house."

"Good idea," I said.

"See you later, Madeline."

Denisha put on her helmet and hopped on behind Austin. They called good-by and rode off across the field. As the roar of the four-wheeler receded in the distance, I sank down in a rocking chair with a relieved sigh. The sun was almost down, and the evening star gleamed above the trees. Jerry brought me a glass of tea and an empty-looking bag of cookies. He shook the bag. "I think they left you one or two, or I can fix supper."

I took the glass. "For once, I'm not hungry. The day has caught up with me."

He sat down on the railing. "It's been pretty intense. Want me to call Shana, or do you want to tell her? She's not going to be happy we broke her husband."

"Maybe it would be better if Hayden tells her what happened," I said. "I get the shakes every time I think what a close call that was."

Jerry didn't say anything for a long moment. I knew what he was thinking.

"She sold you out," I said.

"This con was too big for her. I should have known."

"Hayden could have been killed. You could have been killed. Big Mike is the one who should take care of this. I don't care how many favors it costs me."

"No more favors," Jerry said. "I'll do everything I can to get Big Mike here as soon as possible, Mac. We'll work this out."

CHAPTER TWENTY

I didn't think I would be able to sleep, but the minute Jerry and I fell into bed, I was out. But I did wake earlier than usual Wednesday morning and my mind went into overdrive.

During the fear and excitement surrounding Hayden's abduction, I hadn't had time to spare a moment for Roxanna's challenge and the missing paintings, but with Hayden safely asleep in the guest room and Jerry agreeing to contact Big Mike, my mind took off in the direction of the theft. It was as if my thoughts were running around like the Elmores' little dog Dixie, flinging themselves against the locked door of my brain.

Ten paintings had been stolen from the gala. There were ten paintings from the museum's Thirties collection in Roxanna's exhibit. It occurred to me that was quite a coincidence, especially as she had so many to choose from. Why choose only ten?

Then it hit me: Roxanna's specialty was *tromp l'oeil*, like the mural at the safe house with its painted door that hid a real door. The paintings in her exhibit were all different sizes, like the paintings in the gala, and had all been framed in thick matching frames. Was it possible the missing paintings were *behind* the ones in the display? That she'd chosen Thirties paintings that matched the sizes, or were slightly larger than each gala painting, placed the gala paintings in their frames behind and painted the thick frames in her *tromp l'oeil* style to disguise the fact each painting hid another?

I nudged Jerry awake. "We need to get to the museum."

He pushed his hair out of his eyes. "What, now?"

"As soon as it opens. Can someone cover your shift this morning?"

He yawned. "Sure. Did you have a breakthrough on the case?"

"I hope so," I said. "I'll alert Jake. It's time for a very special episode of *From Crown to Crime.*"

***

Since there was no chance in hell I would leave Hayden alone, or the kids if they stopped by, I called Rusty to see if he was available to stand guard.

"On my way," he said.

Once Rusty was parked on the porch, Jerry and I drove to Parkland where Jake met us at the museum, cell phone in hand. I'm not sure what was brighter, his shirt or his eyes.

"Time to bust this case wide open?" he asked.

"Have your special watch ready."

"You bet."

Once inside, we made our way to the Parkland Museum of Art in the Thirties exhibit. I took out my cell phone and scrolled to the photos of the missing paintings. Then I walked along the hallway, comparing the sizes of the ten paintings to the ones hanging on the walls.

Letticia had mentioned that Roxanna worked day and night to get the exhibit ready. Probably so, if she was going through the museum's collection of paintings from the Thirties, finding just the sizes she needed. I was going to see exactly how special her talent was.

I'd brought along my palette knife. I slid the knife gently along the side of the first painting's frame. A layer of paint came up, then another. As I continued to carefully push my way through the layers, I could see where Roxanna had painted the side of the larger frame. Behind that frame was another painting, still in its original frame, Tully's *Mountain Vista 2.*

"Wowzers," Jake said. "So that's where they are!"

"Yes," I said. "Thank God she didn't paint over them. She just placed each one, frame and all, behind a larger painting and painted up the sides of the frames to hide them. She matched the color and shape of the larger frames perfectly so both frames looked like one."

He moved alongside me as I worked on the second painting, finding *Crystal Coast* behind the picture of the railway station, *Symphony in Pastels* behind the scene of boats, and then, to my immense relief, *Blue Moon Garden* in its silver frame behind the picture of workers at the printing press. Except for brown paint along the sides of the frame, all the gala paintings were unharmed.

"No one would have ever found them," he said.

"No, they wouldn't," came Roxanna's sharp voice. "What the hell are you doing here? And you," she spoke to Jake. "If you know what's good for you you'll shut off that phone." She stood at the end of the hall, blocking my way. Jerry casually backed away and took a watchful position to the side.

Jake put his phone in his pocket and also backed away, both hands up. "Yes, ma'am."

"I don't think the museum will appreciate your vandalism, Madeline."

I had propped the freed paintings against the wall. I turned *Blue Moon Garden* toward her. "Perhaps you'd like to explain how the missing paintings got behind other paintings?

"I'm just as surprised as you are."

"I'm not that surprised," I said. "You're the 'real artist,' aren't you? It must have given you a lot of satisfaction to use your skill to damage Letticia's reputation. You've taken every opportunity to discredit Letticia. It would have been very easy for you to take the grant proposal off her desk. You knew the expensive painting by Halsey was a fake. You called and canceled the playground equipment. Then there's the revenge affair with her son."

She made a noise that might have been a laugh. "I had that boy so scared he was willing to do anything. So weak. Although he was reasonably good in the sack."

"What about the fire at Phoebe's studio?"

"Oh, you can't blame me for that. It always looked like a fire waiting to happen."

"That night Zack brought Phoebe into the museum. He and

Phoebe saw you taking down the gala paintings. Only he was too much of a coward to confront you. But Phoebe wasn't afraid to ask you."

"So what if I did? Why, I could just as easily say that you took the paintings so you could have all the glory of solving the theft. What wonderful publicity for your pitiful little detective agency."

"Nobody would believe that."

She smirked. "Oh, I could make Letticia believe it. She's very easy to manipulate. It was no trouble to convince her that an exhibit called 'A Walk Back in Time' would be perfect for the museum. She's always been a push over for historical recreations. I knew exactly which time period I wanted. The museum has quite a lot of paintings from the Thirties, and naturally, I am familiar with all of them. I knew I'd be able to find ten paintings in the sizes I needed. I simply borrowed the gala paintings, placed them behind the larger paintings, and painted up the edges of the frames so there appeared to be only one frame per picture. Quite easy for someone with my experience and artistic skill in *tromp l'oeil.* They turned out rather well, if I say so myself."

"Because you're the real artist, right?"

"Exactly. I can't tell you how many times my work has been belittled or ignored. I'd had enough rejection. I decided I'd get even." She smiled her unpleasant smile. "At a suitable time, I planned to 'find' the missing paintings, the final proof of Letticia's incompetence, but that time could be today. You've complicated things a bit, but there's no way you can prove anything."

I glanced at Jake, who gave me a grin and a nod.

Roxanna misinterpreted our exchange. "Oh, whoever this man is, if he says anything, I'll sue him for defamation."

Jake's grin widened. "I don't have to say anything. You've said it all. Ms. Deluca, you are the star of the series premiere of *From Crown to Crime.* Congratulations."

For the first time, there was a crack in her resolve. "Who the hell are you?"

"Jake Banner, *Galaxy News Weekly.* Turned off my phone, like you asked me, but you didn't say anything about my watch." He indicated the device on his wrist. "I've got everything right here."

"Why should I believe a trashy tabloid reporter?"

"Because this trashy tabloid reporter also used his watch to call the police. They should be here any minute now. They're gonna love this show." He pressed a button on his watch and Roxanna's voice sounded clearly.

"I knew I'd be able to find ten paintings in the sizes I needed. I simply borrowed the gala paintings, placed them behind the larger paintings, and painted up the edges of the frames so there appeared to be only one frame per picture."

"There's lots more," Jake said cheerfully. "I got everything."

I've repeatedly said I deplore Jerry's past schemes, but the look on Roxanna's face when she realized she'd been conned made me understand the kick he got out of fooling people.

Roxanna turned and ran. She might have made her escape if it hadn't been for Jerry, who anticipated her move, quickly stuck out his foot, and tripped her. She slid onto the polished floor, taking down a side table and a vase of flowers, along with a small bust of someone I hoped wasn't very famous. As she struggled to her feet, Jerry grabbed her by one arm and Jake grabbed the other. She shrieked and cursed as they hauled her up.

This was enough commotion to bring docents, patrons, and Letticia hurrying up to see what was going on.

"These men attacked me!" Roxanna cried. "Call the police."

"Then it's a good thing the police are here," Letticia said. "They'd like to talk to you."

"Great timing," Jake said. "I got the whole story right here." He turned the full beam of his grin to me. "I tell ya, Madeline, this is YouTube gold."

***

Before I did anything else, I took *Blue Moon Garden* out to my car and locked it safely away. Then I went back to Letticia's office.

We sat down. She reached into the top drawer of her desk, took out her checkbook and wrote a check for me. "Thank you, Madeline. Here's the rest of your fee, plus a bonus." She was back to her calm self, looking serene and put together in her severe gray dress, her silver hair contained once again in its neat bun. "I'll contact the other artists and let them know their paintings have been found, and you're the one to thank for finding them."

"I hope you'll understand that I'm keeping *Blue Moon Garden* with me."

"I'll be surprised if you ever let it out of your sight again. I also wanted to tell you that Zack came by yesterday and we had a very honest conversation. Naturally, I was not happy to learn about his affair with Roxanna, but I see now what she's capable of, and I have to admire him for having the courage to tell me. I like to think this whole experience has helped him mature."

I was surprised Zack had found his courage. "That's good to hear. How is Phoebe doing?"

"She's moved in with Zack, and the two of them are going to rebuild her studio. That's part of what Zack wanted to tell me. He was afraid I might not approve because of all this horrible business with Roxanna, but none of that is Phoebe's fault. Roxanna never showed much interest in her daughter, at all."

"Why is that, do you know? Phoebe seems to be a very pleasant person, if a bit scattered."

"The only reason I can think of is because Phoebe looks like her father, and Roxanna's relationship with him was disastrous. Plus Phoebe never was the fiercely ambitious woman Roxanna wanted her to be." She paused as if deciding what to say. "Zack didn't turn out the way I thought he would, either, but that doesn't make me love him any less. Are you and Jerry planning to have children?"

"We've discussed it."

"You'll find out you can plan all you like, but your child will choose his or her own path, and as much as it hurts sometimes, you have to let that child choose."

I thought of my mother's plans for me and how I'd fought against them. I thought of my plans for my mother and how she'd surprised me. "I hope I'll be as understanding as you."

Her smile made her look years younger. "You'll figure it out."

***

Jerry and I were on our way out of the museum when I had a surprise phone call from Officer Jordan Finley.

"Just finished talking with Ms Deluca. I believe I owe you," he said. "I'm not sure we would have figured out the artistic way she hid the paintings."

"Jerry and I saw a silver car leaving Applestone just before Phoebe Deluca's studio went up in flames," I said. "I'm almost certain the car belongs to Roxanna."

"We'll look into that."

"Thanks," I said. "I'm pretty sure her daughter will cooperate with you. You can also talk to Zack Turner. And if you'd make certain Jake Banner of the *Galaxy News Weekly* gets the museum story, I'd appreciate it."

"No problem. Mr. Banner's evidence was most welcome."

Then I called Mom to let her know she could safely return to society.

"*Roxanna* was behind all this?" she said. "Why, for heaven's sake?"

"Seems she and Letticia had a long-standing feud, and this was her way of getting back at her."

"Roxanna Deluca was behind the museum robbery and you found *Blue Moon Garden*? You found all the paintings? I can't believe it."

For a moment, my perverse side said, You can't believe Roxanna's the culprit, or you can't believe I found all the paintings? "That's right."

"Well, I have lots of people to call," she said. "This is astounding news."

And she hung up. No "Thank you, Madeline," or "Great job" or "I knew you could do it."

Did I really expect anything like that?

***

When we got home, the Corvette was gone, a gleaming motorcycle parked in its place. Wallie sat on the porch with Hayden.

She lifted a hand in greeting. "Letticia Booth just called to tell me you found *Fire on the Mountain* and all the other paintings. That's terrific, thanks!"

"You're welcome," I said.

"She said the paintings were hidden behind other paintings, which is actually kinda cool."

"Behind other paintings? I want to hear all the details," Hayden said.

Jerry and I sat down in the remaining rocking chairs, and I explained how Roxanna had used her special art technique to hide the stolen paintings and how Jake's super deluxe techno-watch had recorded her bragging confession to the crime.

"That's great news," he said. "Is *Blue Moon Garden* all right?"

Jerry brought my painting out of the car and turned it so Hayden and Wallie could see. "Stunning as ever."

"And going right back where it belongs," I said. "Where's Rusty?"

Wallie gave Hayden's shoulder a little pat. "Rusty had to go do something, so he called me to come stay with Hayden."

She had on a tight halter top and very short cut-off jeans and was sitting close enough to Hayden that her bare leg was touching his. If Shana drove up right now, this would take a little more explaining than I was prepared for.

Wallie waved a piece of paper. "Have you guys seen this? This is beyond amazing! It's an actual poem about us. Listen to this. It's called 'Ode to the Streetwise Warrior Women.'

"With jets of flame and thundering engines, the warrior women descend on the unwary.

Our hearts beat with the rhythm of a thousand streets.

Our blood is as black and fierce as dinosaur blood.

Our strength reaches back beyond pioneer, beyond crusader,

Beyond the conquerors of the world.

We dare, we fight, we ride."

We roar, I almost added. "That is truly beyond amazing."

"It's almost finished," Hayden said.

Wallie handed him the paper. "I think it's great like it is. I want it tattooed on my back."

Hayden didn't have a reply to this. I'm sure it never occurred to him that people would want to wear his poetry.

Wallie continued to confound him with her next statement. "It's certainly different from your usual stuff."

"It's the least I can do," he said.

She got up and gave Hayden a little hug. "Well, Madeline and Jerry are here, so I'll go. I want to tell the other girls about our poem. When do you think you'll be done? The pageant's tomorrow."

"It'll be ready by then."

"Okay. See ya there. Thanks again, Madeline. The Angels will be really happy to hear you found my painting."

She skipped down to her motorcycle and roared down the drive.

Jerry reached for the battle poem and read it again. "You're slipping, pal. It's not obscure, at all."

"I'm going through an accessible phase."

"Let's see how that works for you. Shana's due tomorrow, right? She'll like this." Jerry caught my eye. "Too bad she missed Valkyrie Waltrauta."

"Have you told her about your arm?" I asked Hayden.

"I thought I'd better wait. I wasn't sure how to explain. 'Oh, by the way, some guys carried me off to a deserted house and broke my arm' didn't sound good no matter how I said it."

My phone beeped with a message. "Okay, guys," I said. "Jake's sent a teaser for the premiere episode of *From Crown to Crime*. Are we ready?"

"I know I am," Jerry said.

I pulled my rocking chair over so he and Hayden could see my phone. *Madeline Maclin: From Crown to Crime* began with my pageant introduction interspersed with scenes of my mother's pageant collection, then switched to a close up of the Madeline Maclin Investigations sign on my office door, followed by the last part of the intro.

"Follow me as I show you how my beauty queen experience prepared me for this fascinating and difficult job."

"So far, so good," Jerry said. "I like that."

"You look very professional," Hayden said. "I'd hire you."

Jake had recorded a voice over for the next scenes of the Eberlin House and my artwork. "But Madeline's day is about to take a serious turn. As she investigates the theft of artwork from the Parkland Museum of Art, including the theft of her own painting, *Blue Moon Garden*, Madeline learns that the director of the museum may have been framed! It's on the museum to search for clues!"

"Okay, that's a little cheesy," Jerry said. "I think you should do your own voice over. Jake makes everything sound tabloid."

I'd already punched Call Back. "I'll tell him that right now."

"No problem, Madeline," Jake said. "That's a much better idea. After all, it's your case, your story. What do you think of the intro? Looks classy, huh? When can you do the voice over for the rest? I've got scenes from the museum, Tully Springfield's, Phoebe's workshop burning up, the big reveal when you found the paintings, Roxanna screaming, loads of footage. We were running around everywhere. Plus you've got to tell me all about the big rescue out at Bylow's Farm. Too bad I missed all that action."

We did run around everywhere. "Maybe tomorrow? I'm taking a little break."

"Sure, sure. But call me if you think of anything else."

I put my phone in my pocket. "You know, I had my doubts about this show, but it's going to be all right."

Jerry pulled me in for a kiss. "Madeline Maclin, YouTube sensation."

CHAPTER TWENTY-ONE

We spent the rest of the day out on the porch. I had phone calls from Tully and the other artists, thanking me for finding their paintings. Around five, Hayden was tired and we convinced him to go upstairs. I promised to bring him dinner as soon as Jerry cooked it.

Jerry started for the kitchen and was halted by the huge shiny black Hummer that pulled up under the trees. He didn't need to tell me whose Hummer that was. Big Mike stepped out, regal and imposing in a gray suit and dark blue tie. Diamonds winked in the twilight from his tie clasp and ring.

"Madeline, Jerry. I believe you wanted to talk to me."

"Yes," I said. "We certainly do. Please come in." Big Mike wouldn't fit comfortably in one of the rocking chairs, and I didn't want him to sit on the porch steps in his elegant suit.

Jerry held the door for us, and Big Mike followed into our living room. He settled on the sofa. "First things first. You'll be glad to know those two men Caldwell hired have been taken care of. They won't bother you again."

I didn't want to think about what that meant. I sat on the other end of the sofa, and Jerry took the white arm chair. "What about Caldwell?" I said. "What about Susie? And most importantly, what about Jerry? We can't spend the rest of our lives wondering if someone with a grudge against you is going to come after him."

"I agree," he said. "I am making plans to eliminate that possibility. Perhaps I was too complacent. Perhaps I put my faith in the wrong people. That won't happen again."

What could I say? I had to believe him. "Thank you."

"I understand you've had a bit of excitement here, villains captured, paintings recovered." He indicated *Blue Moon Garden* back in its rightful spot over the fireplace. "Including your fine work. I trust Mr. Amry is all right."

"He's fine," Jerry said, "But when his wife comes back to pick him up, Mac and I may have a little explaining to do."

Big Mike chuckled. "It will be interesting." More diamonds winked as he adjusted his cuffs. He smiled at me. "Madeline, I must thank you again for introducing me to your mother. I trust if you have any concerns, you'll feel comfortable discussing them with me."

"Everything that's happened with Jerry has made me very uncomfortable," I said. "If the wrong people, as you say, come after you, how do I know you'll be able to keep her safe?"

"Madeline, I keep my private life separate from my business affairs. I assure you I will do everything in my power to protect Cecille."

"And about these business affairs, affair," I said. "This is the happiest my mother has been since I won the Miss Parkland Pageant. But we need to tell her the truth before things get too—" I couldn't think of a tactful word.

"Complicated?" he said. "I agree. When the right time comes, let me handle that. Fair enough?"

I reminded myself that my mother was well able to take care of herself, and if he told her the truth and she didn't like it, she'd say so. "Yes," I said. "Fair enough."

"I'm glad to hear you say that. She's delightful company. I've invited her to join me on my next trip to Paris."

Part of me gave a little "eek!" I hoped my expression stayed calm. "She'll enjoy that."

"She hasn't said yes yet, which is all right. I like a cautious woman. But I believe she'll agree. I've also worked out a little arrangement with the museum."

"An arrangement?"

"I should say sizable donation. I've always been a fan of contemporary art. The Crown Exhibit Hall has a nice ring to it, don't you think?"

Again he chuckled, and Jerry grinned. Okay, so maybe "Crown" was an inside joke for the two of them, but if it benefited the museum and made Letticia look good, then let them have their fun.

At the risk of owing Big Mike another favor, I said, "Now that you have a museum, I don't suppose you'd like to buy an outdoor drama?"

"A rival outdoor drama," Jerry said.

He leaned back. "Sounds intriguing. What's the story?"

Jerry explained about the two Emmaline productions and how a spiteful Amanda had coerced her new husband, Anderson Stratton, into a takeover plot.

"Celosia's show is okay because the Women's Improvement Society has enough money to back the drama, and they don't want to sell, but Stratton is putting pressure on the folks in Rossboro."

Big Mike rubbed his chin. "What's his offer?"

"A hundred thousand."

"So if he owns the play, his wife gets to be the star. That's been done to death, hasn't it?"

The mention of death made me uneasy. I didn't want Big Mike to make the Strattons disappear. "We just want Rossboro to keep their show, that's all."

"Are they going to sell?"

"I know someone who might have the answer to that question." If she hadn't already imploded.

"Tell this person there's been a counter offer."

Joanie will flip, I thought as I punched in her number.

Joanie's voice was on the edge of hysteria. "Oh, Madeline, I'm so glad you called! The playwright is seriously considering taking Stratton's offer! I told you no one can resist that kind of money!"

"Calm down," I said. "There's been a counter offer."

"It's just too much to pass up! You'd have to be completely—what? What are you talking about?"

"Someone else has entered the competitive field of outdoor drama." I glanced at Big Mike, who held up two fingers. Two? I mouthed, shocked. He grinned and nodded.

"Joanie, the offer from the new buyer is two hundred thousand."

I'd never known Joanie Raines to be speechless. After several moments of silence, there was a gasp and a squeak. "Two hundred thousand! Good lord, you must be joking! Who's the buyer? What does he want? What sort of conditions?"

"Let the playwright know and call me back."

Joanie's laugh was sudden and triumphant. "I will! Thanks, Madeline!"

I ended the call. "Big Mike, are you serious? That's an awful lot of money."

"This drama is in Rossboro, right? Do they have a theater?"

"Yes, and an amphitheater."

He spread his large hands as if imagining a scene. "The Crown Center for the Performing Arts."

He and Jerry laughed. I had to join in. "If you keep this up, you'll own the entire county."

"Not a bad idea, Madeline."

Within ten minutes, Joanie called to say the playwright was ecstatic, Stratton had bowed out, and Amanda was furious. "What a wonderful day! Now, how do we get in touch with this buyer?"

"He prefers to remain anonymous, but he does have a few requests," I said. "I'll be acting as his agent. Your show can go on as planned. I'll call tomorrow with more details."

"He doesn't have a wife or a girlfriend he wants in the show, does he?"

"No. You're safe."

"Madeline, you're the best! Thanks so much!"

Now if Anderson Stratton has any sense, he won't attempt a third production, I thought. *Not if he can be outbid at any time.* I put my phone away and looked up at Big Mike's bland smiling face. "Two hundred thousand dollars?"

He shrugged. "I wouldn't have done it if I didn't want to. Now Jerry and I can see which Emmaline comes out on top."

I was beginning to understand that everything was a game to him, not just the cons and schemes, but everything. "Well, I certainly appreciate it."

"Although," he said with a significant look at Jerry, "I do expect dinner."

***

Jerry made fried chicken with rice and gravy, green peas with carrots, and flaky little crescent rolls. For dessert, he fixed brownies with chocolate icing. I took a tray up to Hayden, who was awake and writing in his notebook. He looked up.

"Denisha was right when she said I'd have lots of new things to write about. I've been bombarded with ideas."

"Got one about zombies?"

"Not yet, but give me time." He set the notebook aside for the tray. "I'm really glad you brought me some of that chicken. The smell has been so delicious."

I handed Hayden a stack of napkins. "Need any help?"

"I can manage, thanks. Who's downstairs?"

"Jerry's mentor, Big Mike. He's just saved Rossboro's Emmaline drama." I didn't want to think about how Big Mike earned all that money. "You know Shana comes home tomorrow. Is there a particular version of your adventure you want to tell her?"

"This is Celosia. She's bound to hear something about it. I'd better tell her the truth, which is I don't remember a lot of what happened."

"It'll be better if you're awake and looking as alive as possible." I said. "I'll be back to get the tray."

We chatted until Big Mike had to leave. I thanked him again for all his help.

"Oh, I'll be around," he said. "Jerry, a word, if you will."

Jerry followed Big Mike to the porch. They stood for a while, talking in low voices, until Big Mike gave Jerry a pat on the shoulder and returned to the Hummer.

Trusting Jerry to share any important information, I went upstairs to get Hayden's tray. He was asleep, his notebook in his hand. I couldn't help but notice some lines he'd written. The first was about his unfinished cycle of poems.

It sat like a tangle of multicolored thread. I longed for the patience and inclination to undo it. Now it comes undone and spools wavering ribbons of inspiration so fast I can't catch them all.

The second could only have been about Shana.

After wandering for miles in darkness and deep snow, your presence is the warm red glow of a fire. I sink into your flames, gratefully consumed.

He was back on track.

***

My first phone call Thursday morning was from Jake.

"Check out the front page of the *Herald* today, Madeline! 'Board Member Charged With Theft'! Not the most colorful headline, but it's my story, my byline! I've got a meeting today with the editor, and I know I can talk him into a job. Couldn't have done it without you, Miss Parkland."

"I couldn't have caught Roxanna without you. Thank you."

"We make a good team, huh? Ace Reporter and Pageant PI. Hey, that would make a great show, wouldn't it? I haven't forgotten *From Crown to Crime*. I'll send you the first episode today for you to approve. Gotta go."

With a little assistance from Jerry, Hayden managed to shower and put on a clean shirt and jeans and joined me for breakfast on the porch. Jerry made cheese toast and bacon before hurrying off to Deely's.

I looked out across the peaceful field that surrounded our house, thinking of that wild ride into the woods to rescue Hayden. I wondered if Susie had gotten away, and if Caldwell was still plotting against Big Mike's organization, or if Big Mike had made his rival disappear. Then I thought of Phoebe Deluca and what she'd said about her mother. She'd said, "I only wanted her approval." I understood that so well. For a long while, I wanted to impress my mother, I wanted her acceptance. I had to admit that on some level, I still did. I felt sorry for Phoebe, but wouldn't it be a relief to have the mother you could never please out of your life?

Hmm. Better think through that again. But at least I knew my mother loved me.

"You're thinking awfully hard this morning," Hayden said.

"Care to hear 'Ride of the Valkyries' while you decompress?"

"Because it's so mild and soothing?"

"And victorious."

"I'm okay," I said. "You are, too, I believe."

He was still okay when Shana arrived later that morning just after Jerry got back from his breakfast shift. When she saw Hayden, she stopped dead still in the front yard before dashing up the steps.

"Oh, my God, what's this? What happened?" She hugged him as closely as she could. "Were you in a wreck? Are you hurt anywhere else? What did the doctor say?"

"I'm okay," he said. "Just a broken arm. Madeline's case got a little crazy."

She fixed him with her tawny eyes. "Tell me."

I explained about the missing paintings and all the events that led up to the old house on Bylow's Farm. Hayden took over at that point, telling her some men mistook him for Jerry and carried him off.

"Fortunately, Austin saw everything, and Madeline's Pageantoid Rusty and Helen's Angels came to the rescue. We were all safely out of the house before it fell in."

She stared. "Fell in? You were in a house that collapsed?"

"*After* we all got out. It's important you remember that."

"I can't believe any of this. What do you mean by Madeline's Pageantoid?"

"Rusty's a big fan of Miss Parkland."

"And Helen's Angels? Who are they?? Why were they there?"

"They are real live Valkyries, only with motorcycle helmets instead of horned helmets. I've written a poem for their pageant."

Shana's eyes had gotten progressively larger. "A poem? You've been writing?"

"Yes, I've been writing all day, ever since I got here, really, and this morning, I can't keep up with the ideas. Oh, you know Denisha Simpson, don't you? I've been helping her with her poetry, and she and I have started our own production company. She's got a lot of talent. I'm arranging a book signing for her at Georgia's."

Shana's mouth opened, but no sound came out.

"Things have been a little wild around here," I said.

"I need some tea," she said.

I went into the kitchen and was putting ice cubes in a glass when Shana came in. She looked close to tears.

"Are you okay?" I asked.

She nodded. "He's alive."

"Shana, I'm so sorry. I never dreamed he'd be in any danger here."

"No, he's *alive*, Madeline. He's full of life. He's excited and happy and writing. He's himself again."

"Still, he didn't need to have such a close call."

"It's like you said, you couldn't have predicted that." She took the glass and thanked me.

"You're welcome," I said. "Looks like Hayden's ready to get on with his life."

She beamed at me. "Looks like Hayden's ready for anything."

***

Shana packed Hayden's clothes and put his suitcase in her car. Jerry said he'd drive Hayden's Mini Cooper to their house later and I'd follow in my car. Hayden reminded me about the pageant.

"Wouldn't miss it," I said.

"Don't forget to tell Denisha she can come to my house to work on her poems, or we could continue to meet here, if that's okay."

"I'll relay all your messages."

He grasped my hand. "Thanks for everything, Madeline. I'm going to dedicate my new book to you and Jerry."

The last thing I heard him say to Shana as he got into the car was, "I think I'd like to stop by the animal shelter and see what they've got."

Jerry joined me on the top step and put his arm around my shoulders. "Another successful case solved. I feel like singing a Valkyrie victory song."

"You may yodel 'Hoyotoho' to your heart's content."

I must not have sounded as cheerful as I should. He gave me a closer look. "Something's still bothering you. Is it your mom and

Big Mike?"

"I can't help but be a little concerned."

"Give her a call."

Once again I had to leave a message on Mom's answering machine.

"You want to ride over to her house?" Jerry asked.

"No, that would be taking my concern a little too far. Besides, we've got to put in an appearance at the Miss Streetwise Pageant this afternoon."

"Can't miss that."

"Pageants follow me wherever I go. I don't think I'll ever be truly free."

He laughed. "Now you know how I feel about my old life."

I waited, thinking he'd tell me what Big Mike had said to him on the porch, but he didn't. I would have to wait, but one way or another, I would find out.

Big Mike had saved the museum and the Rossboro outdoor drama, and he'd brought my mother out of her pinched, unhappy life.

I could sit here and worry about things over which I had no control—my usual MO—or I could relax and enjoy what was certain to be a spectacle of lowbrow entertainment.

"You know," I said, "Let me give Jake a call. He needs to see Miss Parkland in all her glory."

I let Jake know where to meet us, and after returning Hayden's car, Jerry and I went to the Miss Streetwise Pageant.

CHAPTER TWENTY-TWO

Streetwise Designs, located on the south side of Parkland, was easy to find. We followed the sounds of revving engines and the heavy thumping of bass guitars and drums to a body shop, garage, and parking lot crammed with muscle cars, motorcycles, and sports cars. Flags flapped in the breeze, and sunlight bounced off the giant earrings, sequined jean shorts, and rows of bracelets and necklaces on the tanned, wild-haired women. The men wore cowboy hats, baseball caps, or bandanas and tee shirts emblazoned with motorcycle logos and beer slogans. Everyone crowded around the stage and runway, bottles and plastic cups of beer in hand, laughing and calling out encouragement to their favorite contestants, who were already lined up and ready to go.

Jake was in tabloid heaven, filming the more outrageous outfits and interviewing the loudest and weirdest of the crowd. He'd been thrilled by my choice of attire. I had decided to embrace the event and wore a short gold gown from my collection of cocktail dresses, matching gold high heels with silver rhinestone straps, all the makeup I'd worn for the introduction to *From Crown to Crime*, and Jake's loaner tiara. Jerry wore a plain blue shirt and jeans, but had selected his best blue tie with yellow and red race cars for the occasion.

Rusty, looming over the crowd, motioned for us to come up to the judges' table where we met a hefty man in green spandex and a top hat decorated with dollar bills who introduced himself as Captain Cash from the World of Mattresses across the street, and a rangy dark-haired man in jeans and a lavender tuxedo jacket who said he was Dwayne Richards, Rusty's business partner.

He shook my hand. "Pleasure to meet you, Miss Parkland. You'll be joining us here, I hope. We could use someone with your inside info."

"I hadn't planned on judging the contestants," I said.

Rusty interrupted. "Our third judge had to be in court today. You'd be doing us a big favor."

"It's all in fun, anyway," Richards said. "We've got prizes for everyone."

"You got all dolled up," Rusty said. "Seems a shame not to let everyone see you. Jerry, you be a judge, too. Now where's Hayden? He's supposed to read his poem."

As Rusty plowed through the people in his search for Hayden, Dwayne Richards offered me his folding chair and went to find another chair for Jerry. Captain Cash obligingly moved over.

"So you're a real live beauty queen, huh?"

"She's also an excellent private investigator," Jerry said. "In case you ever need one."

Captain Cash looked impressed. "I will keep that in mind."

Looking out over the crowd, I caught a glimpse of Shana's red hair and waved. "Over here!"

She arrived in a swirl of blue and green scarves, a fat little white dog tucked under one arm. "Here's our latest addition."

"What is it?" Jerry asked with a grin.

"It's supposed to be a dog. Hayden picked the one that looked the most like a ferret."

The little dog was not the most attractive animal I'd ever seen. Its hair grew in all directions, and it looked cross-eyed. But it wiggled happily when I patted its head. "It's cute in a scruffy sort of way."

"I know," Shana said. "But she's friendly and no one else wanted her, so we had to take her home. Her name is Felicity." She shifted the dog to her other arm. "I'm in charge of her while Hayden reads his poem."

"Is he nervous?"

"A little bit, but I think he'll be okay."

I was concerned about Hayden reading his poem to this crowd, but Rusty quieted them down, welcomed everyone to the pageant, and then introduced him.

"Now, we've got our very own poet, Hayden Amry, here, and he's written a special poem for the pageant, so y'all shut up and give him some respect."

"Ode to the Streetwise Warrior Women" went over very well. When Hayden finished, there were cheers, the honking of many car horns, and a chorus of voices repeating, "We dare, we fight, we ride" until Hayden was pleasantly embarrassed and Rusty made everyone stop.

"Great job, Hayden, thanks."

When Hayden came to the judges' table, Felicity wiggled and whined until he handed Shana his copy of the poem and took the little dog in his good arm. She squirmed so she could lick his face and then settled down, panting.

"My turn," Shana said, and gave him a kiss. "That was really good."

"Yes, congratulations," I said. "You've found a new audience."

Rusty's voice boomed over the speakers. "Okay, now let me introduce our judges for today's competition. All the way from across the street, you know him as a man who sleeps on the job, here's Captain Cash of the World of Mattresses."

Captain Cash stood and tipped his hat to a round of applause.

"Next judge is somebody you all know, and he wants you to know he's gonna be completely impartial even though he's in love with Miss Gear Shift, the design artist behind Streetwise Designs and my good friend, Dwayne Richards."

Richards took a bow and acknowledged the hoots and cat calls from the crowd with a friendly wave of a certain finger.

As usual, I couldn't see Rusty's eyes behind his sunglasses, but his grin was easy to see. "We're proud and pleased to have the real deal with us today, folks. Put your hands together for Madeline Maclin, a former Miss Parkland and her husband, Jerry Fairweather."

Jerry and I stood and gave the crowd our best pageant waves.

"I guess that makes me Mr. Parkland," Jerry said as we sat down.

"All right, y'all ready to see some beauty queens? Here we go with the first annual Miss Streetwise Pageant!"

One by one, to the accompaniment of amazingly loud country music, the Valkyrie women paraded down the runway in very revealing bathing suits, posed, and sashayed back. Two additional contestants, Miss Retread and Miss Realignment, brought up the rear. More cheers, whistles, blaring air horns, and applause greeted each woman.

Talent was next, and it felt good to laugh at all the ridiculous acts the women had decided to perform. Helga, Miss Gear Shift, changed a tire. Wallie, Miss Overdrive, blew the paper off a straw. Orla, Miss Spark Plug, lit a sparkler and held it until it burned all the way down. Sissy and Leeta, Miss Tail Pipe and Miss Lube Job, texted each other. Miss Retread sang an off-key "Happy Birthday," and Miss Realignment stood on her head.

By the end of this round, everyone was laughing so hard, it didn't matter who won, but the judges agreed that changing a tire, if not a talent, was a skill, and we awarded the Miss Streetwise crown to Miss Gear Shift. I agreed to place the plastic tiara on Helga's head. Rusty helped her with the sash, handed her a bouquet of screwdrivers, and she took her victory walk, crying fake tears and blowing kisses.

Hayden introduced all the women to Shana. Several of them had read her books and were excited to meet her. Jake wanted to meet the contestants, too, and they were delighted to be interviewed.

"This is dynamite stuff, Madeline," he told me. "Maybe not for the *Herald*, but excellent footage for your show."

"Did you get the job?" I asked.

"Yeah, I'm on special assignment for a couple of unsolved crimes in the city. I could use a partner."

Jerry put an arm around me. "Mac has a partner. But she's probably available as a special consultant, as long as it doesn't interfere with her investigations."

Jake grinned. "You got it." Something else caught his attention. "Oh, hey, I wanted to talk to that guy in the UFO tee shirt."

Jerry and I left the Amrys and Felicity surrounded by their fans and strolled over to buy hot dogs and chili fries from one of the many food trucks parked in a semi-circle in the parking lot. Rusty signaled to the owner of the truck.

"This is on me. You two get whatever you want. We couldn't have had this shindig without your help. Turned out pretty damn well."

"Thanks for all your help," I said.

"Pleasure to be on the case with you, Miss Parkland." He motioned to his shop. "See anything you like over there, Jerry? I'll give you a good deal."

"My Jeep would look pretty cool with some flaming skulls along the sides."

"Consider it done. Bring it by one day this week and we'll fix you right up."

"Flaming skulls?" I said as we walked back to my car, our hot dogs and chili fries double-bagged. We thought about staying, but the party showed no signs of slowing down, and my part in the show was over. My gold heels were letting me know it was time to sit down and kick them off. "Really?"

"Maybe flaming biscuits would be more appropriate." Jerry unlocked the car and held the door for me. "I think you enjoyed that."

"The pageant? Maybe just a little." I took off the tiara and rubbed my curls. "But I'm ready to go home and sit on my porch."

I must have sounded more depressed than I realized. Jerry handed me the food and got behind the wheel. "It's your mom, isn't it?"

"Yes, I don't know what I'm feeling. It's been strange since the beginning, a big city case with my mother involved. When I called to tell her I'd solved the crime and found all the paintings, I really hoped for a better reaction than, 'I can't believe it,' and 'I have lots of people to call.'"

"Something along the lines of, 'Way to go, Madeline, great job?'"

"Too much to hope for, I guess."

"Then I'll say it. Way to go, Madeline! Score one more for Madeline Maclin Investigations, solving a big case in Parkland,

NC."

"Thanks," I said. "I think I prefer good old-fashioned Celosian craziness."

"You mean demented librarians and ex-witches?"

"Yes, typical small town stuff."

I watched as the streets passed in a never-changing array of strip malls, gas stations, and restaurants until we reached the Parkland city limits. Jerry turned off the main highway onto a two lane road that wound its way for half an hour through the occasional trailer park and scenes of woodlands, farms, and pastures until we came to the "Welcome to Celosia" sign with its rows of feathery red, yellow, and pink celosia flowers planted in front.

"'Population 7,325,'" Jerry read, "and every single one is crazy, just the way you like them."

"Maybe not every single one, but enough to keep me in business."

We took another country road, the one that led about a mile out of town to the Eberlin House. The fields were still bright with wildflowers, a cow or two munching the thick grass. I recalled how I'd found Hayden wandering along this road and how well things had turned out for him. There really wasn't any need for me to worry about how things were going for my mother, now, was there? I could give her a call when we got home.

I didn't have to call. When we got home, Mom was there.

*****

"Isn't that your mother's car?" Jerry asked as we came up our driveway.

My heart gave a strange little lurch. Mom never liked to visit me in Celosia. But there was her beige Mercedes parked in the driveway, and there she was, sitting in one of the rocking chairs. Jerry parked under the trees, and I ran barefooted up the porch steps.

"What a nice surprise! Is everything okay?'

"Isn't that one of your pageant dresses?"

Of course that would be the first thing she noticed. "Jerry took me out to eat."

"Without your shoes?"

"The gold heels are good for thirty minutes, tops."

Jerry brought them to me, swinging them by their sparkly straps. "How are you doing, Cecille? Would you care for a drink?"

"I'm fine, thank you," she said. "I wanted to have a word with Madeline."

"I'll leave you two at it, then." He gave me a kiss on the cheek and whispered, "Good luck" before going into the house.

Mom led the way into the living room and immediately walked over to *Blue Moon Garden*. "Thank goodness you found this."

She stood for a while, gazing at the flowing blue and white petals of the fantasy flowers as if her own thoughts were in a swirl. There was something different about her, something I couldn't place. Thoughtful introspective Mom was someone I hadn't seen before.

After a long moment, she turned to face me. "I don't know what to say, Madeline. I've been so perplexed by your choice of a career, by your decision to leave Parkland and come live in this tiny little town and deal with criminals and con artists and murderers. But I have to admit you've done a very good job. I've enjoyed telling everyone that my daughter solved this case. I—I'm proud of you."

I caught my breath on a sudden rush of emotion. "That means a lot, Mom. Thank you."

She also took a breath, relieved by my reaction. "Well, now, being a private investigator isn't the safest of occupations, so I expect you to take all proper precautions."

"I will, I promise. And Jerry's always here to help me."

"I'm glad to hear that. But if you two have children, you'll have to make some changes to this line of work."

"We will," I said. "If we decide to have children."

"Either way, I plan to be involved, you know that."

I gave her a hug. "I hope you are, Mom."

She hugged me a little longer than usual and then patted my arm. "Just as long as no one calls me Grandma."

"It's a deal."

"Now, I have to go buy some clothes for my trip. I'm going to Paris with Michael, did he tell you? Of course, I'll buy more fashionable clothes when I'm there. I'm very excited about this."

"I'm glad you're getting to travel."

"He wants to remain anonymous, but I can tell you that Michael has given a generous donation to the museum, much more than the gala would have raised. He is quite extravagant. I like that."

"I figured you would. Do you like him?"

"I do. He always knows exactly what to say. He's a complete gentleman, and he's very complimentary about you."

I'm glad I figured into this equation, strange as it may be.

"I never thought I would care for one of Jerry's friends. From what little you've told me, they are all somewhat shady."

Oh, this one wasn't somewhat shady. He was extremely shady. But as long as he was kind to my mother, did I really care? Plus he had promised to tell her the truth—when he wanted to. I had to believe he would.

But my conscience urged me to warn her. I wouldn't feel comfortable until I gave her a head's up. "Mom, I'm so glad you are enjoying spending time with Michael, but you need to know that his line of work may be a little sketchy."

She was not alarmed. "Well, I'm sure there are times when a successful businessman has to bend the rules. You're not saying he has a criminal record, are you?"

I honestly didn't know the answer to that question.

Mom waved away any objections to Big Mike. "All men have their secrets, Madeline. Lord knows your father did."

That reminded me of something I had to ask. Roxanna Deluca had a deep seated resentment for poor Phoebe because Phoebe resembled her father. I couldn't let Mom's good mood go to waste. She had so few of them. "Mom, am I very much like Dad?"

She was still for a long moment. "You look more like him than me, if that's what you're asking."

The question I really wanted to ask would not come out. *Is that why you tried so hard to make me into something else?* Instead, I asked, "Does that bother you?"

"Why should it bother me? You're a beautiful woman, that's all that matters. Good heavens, Madeline, what brought this on? You know I don't like to talk about your father."

"I know things didn't end well between the two of you, and I thought perhaps when you look at me, it brings up certain memories you'd like to forget."

"That's nonsense."

Usually my mother's flat, This is the End of This Conversation statements rile me, but this time I had to laugh. It was nonsense, wasn't it? Just because an insanely jealous woman hated her daughter for such a ridiculous reason didn't mean I had to flip out over a situation which in no way resembled Roxanna and Phoebe's skewed family dynamic, as Mom had so succinctly reminded me. I felt another rush of affection for the austere and prickly woman who cared more about her social standing than about her daughter's feelings. But that was changing. She was changing.

Maybe. But it looked like we were on the right track. A different track. "Can you stay for a while?"

Mom checked her watch. "I really must go."

"Send me a postcard."

She let me hug her again, and then off she went.

As heart to hearts go, this conversation had been amazingly satisfying, so much better than previous talks. I owed Big Mike. I owed him big time.

I went out to the porch to wave good-by. In a little while, Jerry joined me, and we sat down together on the top step.

"So," he said. "Is she going to Paris?"

"Yes."

"How do you feel about it?"

"Still conflicted but leaning towards relieved. She stopped by to make sure *Blue Moon Garden* was all right. Then she said some surprisingly nice things."

"Such as?"

"'I'm proud of you.'"

"Seriously? That's great. She should be proud of you."

"She also said, 'That's nonsense,' when I asked if my resemblance to my father bothered her."

He put his arms around me. "Sums up just about everything

we've been through lately."

I leaned back comfortably on his shoulder. "Got anything from Wagner for this occasion?"

"'The blissful strain is o'er. We are alone. The first and only time since we have met. Now every pent up thought our hearts may own. No rash intruder this sweet hour shall fret.'"

"Sounds awfully calm for the Valkyrie."

"I jumped over to *Lohengrin*." He looked thoughtful. "Lohengrin Fairweather."

I had only one word for this, but I tempered it with a kiss. "No."

End